FLIGHT OF SPARROWS

Flight
of
Sparrows

BY ROY BROWN

Macmillan Publishing Co., Inc.
New York

First published in Great Britain 1972 by Abelard-Schuman Ltd.
Copyright © 1972 Roy Brown

Macmillan Publishing Co., Inc., 866 Third Avenue,
New York, N.Y. 10022
Collier-Macmillan Canada Ltd., Toronto, Ontario
Library of Congress catalog card number: 72–92432
Printed in the United States of America

1   2   3   4   5   6   7   8   9   10

Library of Congress Cataloging in Publication Data

Brown, Roy.
  Flight of sparrows.

  [1. Runaways—Fiction. 2. London—Fiction]
I. Title.
PZ7.B81693Fl   [Fic]   72-92432
ISBN 0-02-714860-2

FLIGHT OF SPARROWS

1

The drizzle, after a dry spell, had spread a film of fine mud on the street surface. As the traffic crept through the unfamiliar town the tires spun glistening patterns like giant spiders' webs. It was dark now. Not far away a clock struck seven.

The two boys stood practically shoulder to shoulder just in the shelter of a dimly lighted, closed chemist's shop. Their damp clothing had a uniform grayness and the shabbiness of rough travel. The luggage they carried was less similar. The shorter boy had a small, neat zip-up bag at his feet. He'd heeled it behind him to make it less conspicuous. His companion was a head taller, bulkier with a flabby strength, his oddly waxy face taking on a reflected sheen from a street lamp nearby. It was a flatly resentful face, eyes darting to and fro in search of an enemy—perhaps imaginary. A soiled, frayed khaki haversack was slung over his

1

shoulder and he would run his finger and thumb up and down the strap as if he were playing some sort of instrument.

The smaller boy, Keith ("Rabbit") Burrows, thought that every town was different because of its buses. These were long, low-slung vehicles of a sickly beige color: they had a squat, alien appearance as though they had been converted to carry short passengers.

Scobie said, his voice continuing what he thought of as an argument, "Ain't no hurry, is there? Did *I* say there was a hurry? We got clear. Easy, just as I said it would be."

"That truck was heading nearly all the way to the Smoke, that's all. Seems a pity."

"You got to box clever. If we'd stayed on the truck they'd have nabbed us in a stinking roadblock. This way, we shake them off the scent. Screws, fuzz—they're stupid, but not *that* stupid."

"Okay," said Keith. "Okay. I was only saying it was a pity, that's all. I mean, in general." He was trying to tell Scobie that he wasn't criticizing him: he should have kept his mouth shut. Scobie was a genius. Scobie was always right. "I hope the rain won't muck up the fireworks."

"It's stopping," said Scobie, catching a few drops with his hand. "We'll scarper in a minute. Second stage of the plan."

The first stage had been dodging Tyson between Metal Work and tea, then scrambling over the wall

2

behind the line of trees, picking up their belongings packed beforehand and hidden among the refuse bins near the delivery entrance. Easy, as Scobie said. Tyson trusted Keith. It never occurred to him that Keith would skip. No doubt he'd trusted Scobie less, but Scobie was with Keith—he'd practically lived in his pocket for weeks. Trusting Keith so much had lulled Tyson into taking his eyes off both of them—too often.

In the doorway, Keith squirmed at the thought.

The truck had brought them twenty miles already. It would be a laugh, Scobie had said—deadpan as usual—to make the break on Guy Fawkes Night. Crowds of kids milling about, the fuzz busy keeping their beady eyes on pillar boxes and bonfires on bomb sites. It didn't matter, Scobie said, if they didn't get to Doreen's for a week. He'd written to Doreen, saying they'd be around sometime. Doreen had a hotel in East London and she'd put them up, Scobie said. Doreen was his sister. She'd look after them, let them lie low.

Plan Two: make their way south, live off the land, see a bit of the world while they were about it, have a good time. They'd earned it, after over a year in that stinking nick. And by the time they got to Doreen's the heat wouldn't be on anymore.

Plan Three: Scobie had plans of his own, he said. So did Keith, didn't he? Wanted to fix that snotty-nosed bastard who had framed him, right?

"Yeah, but I don't care all that much about that," Keith had said during one of their countless little conferences—in the dorm, in the workshop, in a corner

3

of the recreation room. "I just want my case reviewed, that's all."

"You can't do nothing up here in this imitation Alcatraz," Scobie had said. "You got to get clear. It's easier for two than for one. And let's face it, mate. On your own you wouldn't have the guts to pick the lock of a hen coop."

Scobie said it had stopped raining. He headed along the wet pavement toward a cluster of lights, his confidence and bravado infectious but vaguely irritating. "You hungry? I could eat a horse, mate. Let's nick some food."

They had a bit of money, but Scobie wasn't a great spender. At the school he'd hoarded his earnings like a magpie with pretty rings.

The lights represented a few late shops, a cafe with a garish lighted sign outside, an open-fronted delicatessen displaying plastic-wrapped pastries on sloping stalls. Scobie helped himself to several meat pies and a German sausage which he peeled at once and ate in huge, cheek-bulging chunks. He'd hardly paused in his stride. Back in the shadows beyond the shops he thrust a pie at Keith, who would have preferred to have sat down in the cafe and paid for a hot drink.

Scobie went on south, either his sense of direction sharp or with a knowledge of the town he had not disclosed. You never knew with Scobie. Scobie ate three more pies, and Keith one, then they were in the outskirts. Here and there the sky was suffused with firelight and more and more frequently the cloudy base was fragmented with the scatter of rocket sparks.

Keith's legs began to ache. "What now?"

"Maybe later we'll jump a train for a stretch. Or we'll find somewhere to kip. Early yet, though. Who cares? What's the hurry?"

They trudged on until houses gave way to hedges and taller and taller trees were as bare as black skeletons against a fitful moon. On the heath beside them, some way back from the twisting road, people from the village had lit a bonfire. They stood around it, prodding the fuel of broken chairs and bracken, lighting fireworks, laughing, squealing, their faces bright in the flames.

Scobie said, "Let's go and have fun." He swaggered toward the fire, followed indifferently by Keith. Nobody seemed to notice their approach at first. A large man in a fur-collared coat was lighting a Catherine wheel on a rough trellis and a group of small, scarf-wrapped children watched intently as the firework sputtered, then hesitantly began to turn, gathered momentum, spun in a brilliantly colored disc and finally petered out. The bonfire dimmed a little and a youth with a pitchfork prodded the base, recoiling from the sudden spurts of flame and sparks.

Scobie lit a cigarette and sidled closer. On a chair beside the youth was a box of fireworks. Scobie helped himself to one, lit the blue taper with his cigarette end, then, with a sly, underarm flick, threw it straight into a group of kids. There was an explosion, screams, a scatter of frightened figures.

The villagers had spotted the strangers now, all right! A couple of men advanced on Scobie, including Keith in their hostile stares.

"Which of you flung that firework? You burned a little girl's leg, you oafs."

"The fat one did it—I saw him."

"Fetch the law."

"Grab that yobbo first."

Scobie could move when he wanted. He slipped out of the men's grasp and made for the darkness of the heath. Keith dodged after him, not wanting to be Scobie's scapegoat. He ran on until he was sure the villagers weren't bothering to send a posse after them, then stopped, lungs bursting, reckoning that he would never find Scobie in this suddenly moonless wilderness. He couldn't be sure whether he was sorry or glad! Then he heard a faint hiss from the shadow of a farm building. When Keith joined him Scobie said, "We shook them easy." His laugh was hollow, without feeling.

Keith said, "That was daft, chucking that firework. Drawing attention to us like that. Besides . . . ."

"Besides what?"

"Skip it." It was no use expecting Scobie to feel remorse over a kid's burned leg. Scobie said, "I've found a place to doss down."

It was a barn with plenty of hay, mostly loose and smelling of manure. Moonlight leaked through cracks and they groped about making a couple of rough beds. There were bird twitterings and the rustle of a rodent somewhere, but no sounds of pursuit.

"We'll push on early tomorrow," said Scobie, stretching himself out. "I'm not stopping out in the sticks. There's nothing to nick in the country. Who wants to eat stinking berries and that?"

"What'll we do? Catch a train?"

"Yeah, could do worse."

There were a couple of the pies left. Keith thought Scobie flung him one a bit grudgingly. He didn't fancy it much, so he flung it back. Keith checked through his bag, changed his damp socks, laid out a spare shirt to use as a pillow. He felt utterly tired but he didn't want to sleep till Scobie did. Scobie was smoking and Keith had the crazy feeling that if he gave way to his exhaustion Scobie would set fire to the barn—either by accident or for kicks—and the anxiety clung to him like wet clothes.

Scobie went into a ruminative mood. "We don't have to stick here, really. We could go to a hotel, if we was near a decent burg. One of them posh hotels with lights at the front. Nothing to it. You go in the foyer and look the booking clerk straight in the eye, as if he'd just crawled in under the skirting board. You dream up a spiel of some sort. You've come on ahead of your uncle who's just docked in Liverpool and wants two rooms for the night. Good rooms, with showers, and windows looking out on trees."

Scobie drew on his cigarette, shed sparks on dry straw. "My sister Doreen, she's got a hotel. I told you. She's all right is Doreen. She'll see we're all right."

Scobie flung his cigarette end out of the door at last. Instead of settling down, though, he went out after it, slamming the door, treating Keith as if he suddenly weren't there.

Keith gave up and fell asleep almost at once. He dreamed that Scobie was laughing, as he'd done when he'd told Keith what he ought to do to Turner—his eyes as cold as ice. Then, sometime during the night, Keith woke with the awareness of Scobie's tossing form beside him just as if they were both back in the dorm. Scobie mumbling, Scobie restless as a wave.

An owl hooted. A distant dog barked.

Keith had a stomach ache and his head was full of a dull pain. It was partly the running away. What would his mum feel when she heard? At this rate there was not a chance of reaching her before the coppers did. And it was partly letting Tyson in the cart, betraying his trust. Keith wriggled uncomfortably, thinking of Tyson, thinking of his mum again. She'd have kittens when she found out he was missing. She'd wait for him, sitting up all night by the front-room window. When he crept in at the back door she'd give him hell; then she'd dish out eggs and beans and thick bread and butter, and by the time he'd finished she'd be smiling as if she couldn't help it.

But London was still a long way off, and Keith *couldn't* go home even when he got there. He was stuck with Scobie—as usual—and Scobie was calling the tune.

2

The fire was at its height: a crackling shell of orange and red and white and spitting shafts of indigo—a gigantic, strange flower in full bloom. Sparks whirled into the black sky, gyrating in free patterns, in woven fantasies of fire specks. The pink faces, those not hideously masked, were turned toward the bonfire, then to the sky, then to the sudden spurt of a new firework in the grass.

Sprog wandered about in the brightness and shadow. His dirty face was pink. He joined in the startled laughter. He gasped and blinked. His eyes joined the others' in parabolic wonderment as a rocket spumed across the sky.

Nobody had noticed that Sprog had joined the Guy Fawkes party on the green: a sloping piece of wasteland in East London, above the canal. In a way it was like coming home—a sort of home—and the warmth was like walls and the voices had a familiar, friendly ring like those of people who cared.

Sprog remembered that he'd left his duffel bag by a seat at the edge of the green. It was a frayed, much soiled, much traveled piece of luggage with the faded name of a celebrated football team stenciled on the side. He did not reckon anyone would want to pinch it.

Suddenly a dog ran out of the shadows into the firelight. It was not large, but not all that small either. Just a tufty nondescript mongrel excited by the noise and light—and it was limping as it dragged something along, holding a strap in its teeth, the weight of the object forcing it to cut a crazy, sidelong course across the green. A bundle, a bag . . . a duffel bag! At the bonfire the mongrel behaved as recklessly as a moth around a candle, starting on a spiral run much too close to the flames. Somebody shouted. Somebody tried to trap the bag with an outstretched foot. A posse of children formed itself to give pursuit. The dog eluded them all, leaping and twisting and dodging. Twice it passed close to Sprog, eyes full of fire, and Sprog tried to grab it. The dog raced on.

The children attacked. They flung lighted fireworks, burning sticks, clods of earth, not meaning to hurt. The mongrel was an outcast, a sport, a moving target. It ran the gauntlet, limping awkwardly down the slope into the misty shadows. Even then the children were not content, but herded after it. The game had grown swiftly: here were cavemen hunters bearing torches—only the torches were large sparklers twirled above their heads. Here was ritual, with grotesque masks seen in hideous glimpses as they spread out down the slope.

Sprog panted after them. He cut a diagonal path and arrived first close to the canal bank, not knowing it was there. He saw the mongrel, blinded and confused and frightened, and he saw his duffel bag with the strap apparently still attached to the dog's teeth. There was a tug of pity for the dog, but a clearer image—as if everything was laid out neatly in Sprog's mind for inspection—of the bag's contents. A piece of stale bread, a bruised apple, a bundle of comics, a map he could scarcely read, a broken watch, a flashlight . . . .

No, he had the flashlight in his pocket. He switched it on—dimly because the battery was nearly done—then off again as whoops and jeers came over the brow of the hillock.

"He's gone. The mutt's gone away."

"Drowned hisself in the canal, poor mutt."

"He had somebody's bag in his mouth."

"Let's go on hunting, then."

"Let's get back to the fire."

Sprog crouched among some rubbish and driftwood, looking cautiously upward and backward. He'd just seen the mongrel slink off, deep into the hollow to his right. The children were breaking to the left in a giggling scatter, the sparklers beginning to die but some still sketching silver halos.

Sprog waited. The sky behind him was a pallid pink.

11

It cast a reflection, quivering like flesh, on a surface stretching flat at the very bottom of the slope beyond a broken fence of split willow. Water! A canal, the kids had said. Sprog switched the flashlight back on and groped his way down through a broken stretch of fence, finding himself on a narrow towpath. He felt the breath of moving air on his face and his thin flashlight beam cast a bent ray into sluggishly drifting water.

The dog had slunk off to the right but was biding its time, no breath betraying its presence. There was only the distant crackle of fireworks and the sound of muffled voices from the upper green. Maybe the mongrel had finally lost hold of the duffel bag and dropped it along the towpath, or into the canal where, as the kids had ghoulishly suggested, the dog had gone down with it.

Sprog searched—and searched. And then, now that his eyes had shed the firelight, he could pick out the faint appearance of an arched structure ahead. A bridge over the canal? No, too deep, too dark. Sprog knelt down and tried to peer in. There was nothing to see except the tunnel mouth leisurely drinking the canal water, occasionally gobbling a piece of flotsam. Had it gulped dog, duffel bag and all?

The far side was touched with pink—a pink, mysterious bank with a gaunt structure stretched across it, all girders and the disk of a huge wheel. It stood chunkily beside a low-pitched building with no windows. On the near side the towpath narrowed sharply and became a ledge passing into the mouth of the tunnel. Sprog had just discovered this when there came a single, short, sharp bark from the pitch darkness within. Sprog's tattered sandals groped for a foothold on the ledge and he grasped the brickwork of the tunnel arch and eased himself along, clawing at a damp, mossy wall.

It was crazy, Sprog knew. He'd finish up by getting *himself* drowned—he'd never learned to swim. And in order to use his hands he'd had to stuff the little flashlight back in his pocket. It wasn't worth it—over a duffel bag. Perhaps it was the sting of injustice—having the bag nicked from under his nose; perhaps it was curiosity, a sense of being drawn into a beginning that must have a finish.

He continued along the ledge—a slight, wiry, nimble boy, small for his age. Only his quick wits saved him from disaster a few feet farther along. The plain, even surface of the curved wall abruptly gave way and Sprog plunged into emptiness, stumbled forward, felt as if he were hurling into a chasm—but he came up short against the limits of a recess. He didn't know this until, panting and swearing, he got his flashlight working and saw that he was standing in a larger space with a domed roof of bricks over his head and some wooden crates nearby. He sat down on one of the crates and listened.

There was a splash, the sound of someone or something swimming: that indistinct, licking sound of a living body in water. Sprog's flashlight beam probed the darkness and soon picked up the head of a dog skimming the surface, heading in his direction. When it reached Sprog's side it came easily out of the water and stood there on three legs, one hind leg raised, front paws splayed, shaking itself free of water, turning unexpectedly friendly eyes on Sprog. There was no duffel bag though.

A different light flashed across the canal from the ledge on the other side. When it flashed a second time, Sprog glimpsed a face. Not so much a face as a mask . . . a Guy Fawkes mask? Had one of those kids broken away from the others, come here after the dog? Had he discovered Sprog and decided to play some sort of scary game with him?

Then Sprog saw something else: his duffel bag sitting beside a crate on the opposite ledge. The masked face had recoiled from Sprog's feeble flashlight, but the bag had remained there, leaning wetly against a crate. The face had vanished and Sprog had little interest in it, only in his bag, only in the possessions which were all he had but for the ragged clothes he wore.

It was no more than ten feet across to the ledge. Swim or not, Sprog was determined to retrieve his bag. He gritted his teeth and slipped into the water and his feet found bottom at once. All he had to do was wade across, water almost up to his chin. It was anger, now, which made him forget the coldness of the water, give no thought to the impossibility of getting properly dry afterward. Some kid was baiting him and in

Sprog's world—even allowing for Sprog's normally good-natured temperament—it meant a punch on the nose or, if the other kid was that much bigger, a knee in the groin. The kid in the Guy Fawkes mask, in short, was in for a bashing.

Sprog had new problems, though, out in the middle of the canal's width. He lost his sense of direction, and by now what was left of his flashlight battery was soaked to extinction. Even the faint light from the tunnel mouth was difficult to locate. The glistening surface of the water gave no clue.

Above the contented hiss of water at the tunnel's mouth Sprog heard the dog whine. Sprog was cold—shaking with the cold, absurdly incapable of movement as if he were encased in ice. The cry escaped his lips involuntarily. He was not so much crying for help as marking his position, telling the darkness that he was there.

The light flashed on again and this time was not extinguished. Sprog swiveled his head—without realizing it, he'd turned and started heading back the way he had come—and saw the masked face, with its hideous fixed expression, yet bright-eyed and watchful, set toward him, awaiting him, mocking him.

The kid *wanted* him to come. He had a nerve! The face vanished and after a brief and uncertain flicker the light went out. Sprog was once again in a deep darkness pricked only with specks of faint water-light. He waded on the rest of the way, his teeth chattering, groping for the ledge. He reached it and hauled himself out. A low, threatening growl came from the darkness but the dog did not move.

Once more the flashlight came on, full into Sprog's face, then dipped. Sprog was aware of more crates, the matted figure of a dog squatting beside his soaked duffel bag. And, next to them, the masked boy's eyes locked in his.

"Quit larking about mate," said Sprog, his voice quivering with cold. "That's my belongings you've got there. Your dog nicked them from the green—if he *is* your dog."

The no-answer and the way the small crouching figure didn't move a fraction, not even the eyes, was disturbing. The mask . . . indistinct in that light, infuriating because it gave the boy the advantage of self-concealment. Sprog could have taken his duffel bag without further argument and made his way out of the tunnel. But the mask was a challenge; the boy deserved some retribution, such as having his silly mask ripped off and flung into the water—the water Sprog had endured, which still saturated his clothes and made his eyes smart.

"I'll have *that*, mate," said Sprog, and his hands reached out, grasping, tearing. At the first touch the boy reeled back—not screaming, but emitting a sound that was between a sigh and a cry. Sprog's finger met flesh: warm, living flesh slightly rough and unreal to the touch of his hands.

3

There was a short, shocked moment when Sprog's hands recoiled from the strange, ugly face, then he jumped clean back into the stinking water of the canal.

He went under, staggered upright again, spat out water, was blinded and gasping—and only by chance did he find his own side of the tunnel and clamber onto the ledge, still spitting and gasping into the gray unbroken gloom over the water. He'd lost one of his sandals. Stupidly, Sprog sat there dangling his feet over the wall, hoping the sandal would float back to him. But the lapping water had carried it away, swallowed it up. A stinging pain between two of his bare toes suggested that Sprog had cut his foot on something sharp on the canal bottom.

Across the tunnel the dog barked and fussed again, then a thin flashlight beam jerked agitatedly to and fro, first on the water, then on the brick wall above Sprog's head.

There was a splash. Someone—or something—was swimming across, but it was not the figure holding the flashlight. Almost at the same moment a limp object hit the crate behind Sprog and rolled accurately until it nestled wetly against his spine. His duffel bag! Sprog thumped his little flashlight on the ledge and got it to give out a feeble light which he played on the opposite wall. There was a brief duel of flashlights, then the dog arrived, clambering up beside Sprog, not unfriendly, sniffing faintly and shedding a shower of water. The figure opposite moved toward the tunnel entrance—first a pinpoint of light, then a silhouette. It paused on the narrow ledge linking the towpath with the quay and gave a long, low whistle.

The dog was torn between curiosity about Sprog and obedience to the whistle. Eventually it somehow made its way along the ledge on Sprog's side toward the towpath. Sprog picked up his duffel bag and limped after the dog, no longer afraid, only wanting to be on the move—satisfied that if there *was* anything menacing about the creature he had encountered, at least they were separated by a good strip of canal water.

The sky was still pink above the canal. Outlined against it the figure was climbing up the steep bank toward the streets roofing the canal tunnel. Nearly at the top it paused again, whistled, sending the dog into a frenzy of indecision. The dog barked, leaped into the canal, reached the other side, then stood three-legged and hesitant, barking back at Sprog.

Sprog had his belongings—except for the lost sandal, and that couldn't be helped. Most of him wanted to hoist the duffel bag on his shoulder and get on his way—somewhere. A part of him remained inquisitive, feeling vaguely that he had stumbled on some mystery which he couldn't really walk out on. And there was the dog, that nervy, restless, nimble-witted mongrel adopting a waiting stance on the towpath: *it* was demanding that Sprog stay.

"Oh, shuddup!" Sprog practically yelled across. Then he did hoist the bag and began making his own way up *his* side of the tunnel, up the almost sheer cliff of rough grass and weeds to the roadway above.

It was a narrow, scantily lit street serving an industrial area with no houses. It curved between walls broken by gates, one of which was open, giving a far-off view of the bonfire on the strip of green.

The dog stood on three legs beneath a lamppost shedding a mean light on a narrow pavement. It was looking back at Sprog, and the figure which stood beside it was that of a boy a little taller than Sprog. The boy said nothing. The lamp did no more than suggest the outline of his grotesque face, and there was a stare of bright eyes, then a turn of the head and a turn of the body and it began briskly moving off along the pavement. The dog heeled after him, but every few crippled steps it swung its head round, watching to see if Sprog was following.

Sprog wasn't. He wanted nothing to do with a crippled mutt, even less with the creature from the tunnel. He turned and ran, still dripping wet and shivering, in the opposite direction.

But in a moment he heard the dog's paws whispering on the dark road. "Buzz off!" said Sprog. The mongrel leaped up, badly balanced, tried to paw Sprog's chest and lick his hand. Sprog stuck his bare foot at it and pushed it away. The dog withdrew a few yards, watching Sprog with wounded reproach.

Sprog found a stick and threw it along the length of the street in the direction of the lamppost. The mongrel went after it. By the time it came back with the stick in its mouth, Sprog had found an open gate and vanished across a factory yard. He climbed a wall on the far side, dropped down, and discovered himself in a broader, brighter street busy with traffic.

He went on, keeping close to the shabby shop fronts. At the first alley he'd hide himself—his filth and one bare foot must at any moment invite pity, and pity was dangerous. Pity would carry him straight back to the life he had escaped from, and Sprog would rather be caught in a rattrap.

There was a short, forgiving bark just behind him. Sprog swore, ran on, found the mouth of an alley toothed with white posts. He took cover behind some ashcans, but his scent was stronger than anything under their lids. The dog sniffed, barked, upset one of the cans, sending its lid clattering noisily over the sloping cobbles of the alley. It saw Sprog crouched there, gave a loving "wuff," and stuck its nose affectionately beneath Sprog's chin.

A single feeble light glowed on the wall above in a glass shade attached to a metal hook. It cast a pool of illumination on the rubbish area and at the edge of it the boy stood in silence, watching. "You made me jump, mate," gasped Sprog. "Hey, come and get your mutt off me. I wish you'd both stop follering me about."

The boy neither answered nor moved. There was hurt reproach in that strange stare.

"I don't want him," protested Sprog. "*I* never asked him to come after me." He gave the mongrel a shove to prove it. The dog wouldn't budge. "Whistle him," suggested Sprog. "Call him off. What's his name?"

The boy didn't speak.

"What you done with your tongue, then?" inquired Sprog. "If you can't be civil . . . ."

The boy moved—astonishingly fast, making off into the shadows with an odd, springing gait like a gazelle. A helmet had appeared at the top of the alley. Sprog saw it too, if a trifle late. He ducked down behind the ashcans and held the dog close to him, telling himself that if it so much as whimpered he'd choke it with his bare hands. The dog stayed perfectly quiet. The heavy tread of the constable's footsteps passed rhythmically on the cobbles, not quickening, not urgent. When they had died away Sprog risked a peep over the ashcan lid. The alley was deserted and silent.

Sprog got up, shivering. He didn't want the street, he didn't want to go the way the policeman had. He looked for a way through the backs of the buildings, peering through cracks and over fences. The dog stayed close, but Sprog ignored it.

Sprog eventually found the spot he wanted: a tall, broken fence dividing that part of the alley from an old demolition site. When he jumped over, a late rocket spumed overhead, accompanied by fresh drops of rain. Sprog gingerly made his way across the open space, knowing that he was nearly at the end of his tether. He'd have to find food and shelter soon. He wasn't worried, though. It was a problem he had faced often and something always turned up. Something he could nick, somewhere he could put his head down, maybe wring out his clothes.

The mongrel suddenly left his side and ran off, barking. Sprog was glad, hoping he would lose it now. Dogs were all right, but they could be a dead giveaway. He was better off alone—he was a loner. Maybe the mutt would find the kid okay.

"Heck!" thought Sprog, no longer frightened and only mildly curious, "what a mush!" He meant the kid's face—it was like he'd been in some sort of accident.

Only it didn't explain why he had scarpered off when he'd spotted that copper; and it didn't explain why he'd been hiding in the tunnel. Didn't he have a home around here somewhere? He and the dog . . . . Sprog was suddenly glad that the kid had a dog. A dog wouldn't care about a face.

It was rough, though, thought Sprog, feeling more and more sorry about the kid, wishing he'd found a way of being more friendly—only the kid hadn't even spoken to him, and he'd got the stupid idea that Sprog was trying to steal his mutt.

Sprog was thinking all this and at the same time picking his route cautiously across the site, careful not to step on brambles or rusty cans with his bare foot. Just as he'd hoped, there were some back gardens on the far side, and the fireworks were mostly used up. At this time of evening Sprog would soon find a shed he could open—maybe even one with a bag of apples in it, or at least raw vegetables.

It was then that the mongrel came limping back through the long grass, greeting Sprog like a long lost friend. It scampered off again and Sprog saw the boy, waiting and watching, not twenty paces away. When the boy saw Sprog looking back at him, he loped on toward the fence.

Now the dog ran back and forth between the two of them, as if undecided. As Sprog drew nearer to the boy, the mongrel's journeys became shorter and shorter, until the boys were standing nearly side by side, and all the dog had to do was turn its head toward one, then the other. Sprog could hear the unmistakable swishing of the dog's tail in the darkness.

Then the boy stooped and squeezed through the fence from which a couple of planks had been removed. What the boy could do, Sprog could manage also. So could the dog.

Soon the three of them stood in a street, at the top of a flight of stone steps. First the boy, then the mongrel, then Sprog went down the steps into a deep pool of darkness. Not a word was spoken until, when the boy unfastened a door and pushed it squeakily open, Sprog said, "What's *this* place, then?"

The boy didn't answer. The whites of his eyes were fixed on Sprog for a moment, then there came the brief rasp of a match on a box and the boy lit a little lamp which stood on a table just beyond the door.

4

The freight train they jumped got Keith and Scobie as far as Bedford, but not until the following evening. Too early, and exhausted, they shared a bus shelter in another country area. It was a dismal spot with a cutting east wind howling vindictively through broken side panels. Keith slept only in short stretches and so did Scobie, but they were rarely awake at the same time and when they were they did not speak.

Twice Keith rolled clean off the seat, woke with his mouth slobbering and hands pawing the littered cement floor. He dreamed about visiting his dad's grave. His mum had always wanted him to go with her, rarely one of the others.

"It's quite a nice grave. On his birthday we'll bring some white flowers. White flowers are best. It's more respectful, putting white flowers on a grave. It would have been nice if they'd put him next to Jenny. . . ."

Keith had never seen Jenny except in photographs. She was an older sister who had died when he was a baby. Keith was the eldest now—the eldest of six. The neighbors referred to them all as "the Rabbits," because of the name, Burrows, and because there were so many of them.

Keith's mum could be sentimental, a bit unreal—like she was at the cemetery, prodding the grave with a tiny fork, sniffing back half-real tears. Placing white flowers on a grave was a proper thing to do, like concealing their poverty with careful brushing and darning, and because he was dead Mrs. Burrows contrived to embalm even Keith's dad in respectable memoriam.

She was tough, though, beneath the pretenses. She'd wanted Keith to stay on at school till he was eighteen, maybe go to the university. She was ambitious for Keith. Neither was it a pretense that she knew instinctively Keith was innocent. But, tight-lipped in court, she had adopted a philosophical view of his "sentence."

"You'll learn something, son. Don't be bitter. Behave yourself and try and think of it as boarding school. And don't get into bad company." That was a laugh!

Even while Mr. Burrows had been serving his third spell in prison she had wanted Keith to hold his head high. Whenever he had complained about old Hibbert she had said, "Stand up to him, son. I don't mean be cheeky, but look after your rights."

Against old Hibbert?

"What precisely is this mess on your exercise book, Burrows?"

"Baked beans, sir."

"Are you trying to be funny?"

"No, my little brother upset his tea on it."

"And what exactly was your homework book doing on the tea table?"

There was nowhere else to put it, Keith had thought. Mr. Hibbert didn't like long hair, and he didn't like back-talk, and most of all he took exception to Keith. His mistrust and dislike gave his eyes a cold look whenever they alighted on Rabbit. And a mislaid penknife or a pilfered sweat shirt was enough to bring Keith under that suspiciously ironic scrutiny. His dad, after all, had a record, hadn't he? The last conviction was for robbery, with violence in fact! (Ned Burrows, spotted while shoving a jemmy in a drawer frame, had socked the shopkeeper who had crept up behind him.)

Before daybreak it began to rain again. Scobie woke, sullen and restive, and said, "Let's hoof it—find somewhere better to kip."

They trudged along for a while until their clothing clung to their bodies like sheets of pasted paper. Scobie had found a way of blaming Keith because, he said, they had jumped off the train too soon. They could easily have slipped away at the station and sheltered there for a few hours.

"I could have conned the ticket collector. Done it

often enough. And you can nick a few sandwiches easy from them crowded caffs on the platform."

Keith knew it had been Scobie's idea to jump. According to Scobie, some passengers in the corridor was taking too much interest in them. But Keith rarely argued with Scobie. They crossed a couple of fields before finding the road again. Keith had forgotten the holes in his shoes. He soon felt he'd been squelching barefoot through inches of water all night —water in lush grass concealing stale cows' dung and bramble prickles and rusty tins left behind by an earlier summer's picnickers. Scobie ambled doggedly on. The only time he hurried was when he was in the country, or when he spotted a policeman.

They were on the small bridge ahead, two of them leaning against their parked car with the blue light still blinking fuzzily in the rain. Scobie hesitated and the policemen picked up his arrested movement like dogs detecting the scent of fear. One of them moved forward. "Hey, lad!"

Scobie went to his right and straight over a four-foot wall. His agility and strength had surprised Keith only the first time he'd seen it. Keith followed, but slow-witted, less triggered, almost yielding a sodden shoe into the policeman's outstretched hand. He was aware of falling almost sheer down a deep, deep slope grabbing at coarse wet grass and cutting his hands. His descent ended only when he reached the bottom of the embankment. Then he sat up, panting and bruised. Scobie called him huskily from farther along the hollow. Above, a light swished to and fro picking out raindrops.

The policemen weren't coming down. The flashlight beams, however, moved off in the direction Scobie had taken, stabbing down into the hollow. The police knew the area. If they wanted them they probably had a better means of trapping them than getting their shoes and trousers soaked. Perhaps Scobie sensed it too. He suddenly yelled an oath at Keith and set off into a flat waste to his right. To his horror, Keith suddenly realized that it was the railway. An approaching train lighted up a brilliant crisscross of junction rails, and there was Scobie across the first pair.

The train whistled—maybe the driver had spotted Scobie. Scobie went flat and the roaring, rattling carriages passed within a few feet of where he lay.

The train passed at last and Scobie got up, raced on across, his bulky frame hopping the rails. Far across the junction the cowled eyes of red and green signals watched with disapproval.

The lines seemed clear now, and Keith followed, not daring to look up and down. On the other side Scobie, his cockiness returning, made more slowly toward a tallish building swathed in darkness. He went up wooden steps, stood on the little landing at the top and waited for Keith. When Keith got there Scobie was picking the lock of a door.

The door gave way and they were inside. Half the room was taken up by thigh-high brass-handled levers and a snarl of corroded wires snaking across the floor. Scobie's carefully blinkered light also discovered a bench with nondescript rubbish on it including a half-eaten sandwich as hard as slate and a heavily stained tin mug.

"Used to be a signal box," announced Scobie unnecessarily. His light went on dithering about, finally coming to rest full in Keith's face. "You've cut yourself, mate. A proper mess you look."

Keith dabbed at his face with a soaked handkerchief. Scobie hardly looked immaculate but he'd come through better than Keith. He was more out of breath, though.

"We'll lie low for a bit," Scobie said. His light danced on the two items of luggage. A trickle of water ran across the dusty floor from Keith's case. In following it Scobie spotted a heap of sacks and some tarpaulin. "We'll finish our kip, eh? We shook those coppers. Boy, did we move! Reckon they were on to us?" He thought about it, biting his thumb, the weakness and uncertainty coming back. "That guard on the train saw us, I bet—and put in a report. They're all the same." He meant people in uniform. To Scobie they were all either "fuzz" or "screws"—even traffic wardens. "I don't get how they could've tracked us this far, though. . . ."

He went on talking but you learned to switch Scobie off.

Rain beat on the roof like kettle drums; the thin walls offered the illusion of safety. A little later they sorted out their things and strung bits along the bench to dry. There was nothing to eat, but Keith's stomach wouldn't have taken it if there had been and even Scobie didn't complain.

They made beds of the sacks and tarpaulin. Scobie said, "If there's no fuzz about, we'll push on at daylight. Not that we've got to hurry."

Just now Scobie was relishing his precarious freedom. Freedom for Scobie was a thing in itself. He didn't have to do anything special with it. Scobie fell asleep. From long practice Keith could sense when Scobie's restless consciousness had slipped into the dark. A train hurtled by, its lights flickering past the windows above the layers, and Keith thought about Turner.

It was a long time after Scobie had befriended Keith, in that clinging way he was never sure he'd welcomed or not, that Keith told his story, not expecting to be believed.

"How was it done, then?"

"Turner—the kid I told you about—gave me some money. It was only a quid. I was supposed to mind it for him while he went swimming. It was treated with chemical, as a trap. When they lined us up, me and a couple of the other kids, they found blue stains on our fingers."

"What about Turner's mitts?"

"You're joking. He was too smart for that. He never touched the money after it was doctored. There was a lot more nicked, of course."

31

"How much?"

"Fifty—a bit more."

"Big deal! They sent you up here for that? First offense?"

"Somebody hit Perry. Perry was the oldish teacher who kept the holiday fund—I told you about him. He got a concussion and nearly kicked the bucket."

"You reckon that was Turner?"

"I dunno. Probably somebody else, but he was in on it. Only the two of us were caught. The other three got probation.'

"And you didn't, because your old man was a jail-bird? Where's Turner now?"

"Where he used to be, I suppose. Plaistow—it's in London. . . ."

"I know, I know. I come from the Smoke, don't forget." He'd looked shrewd, then. "You ought to look him up and give him a good doing over, mate. I would."

"Oh, forget it." Keith had shrugged. Even then something in Scobie's tone, in his hooded expression, had made Keith shiver. "Anyway, what can I do, stuck in this place?"

Keith couldn't remember exactly how one thing had led to another: the talk, the plans, the escape . . . not because of Turner at all, in the end, but because Scobie had decided to break and he'd wanted Keith along, and Keith had lost the power to shake his head.

They got away at seven, leaving the railway behind and cutting through a wood sticky underfoot with mud. A few winter birds twittered unwelcomingly and the rising sun shed bits of rainbow through the bleak, tangled trees.

In the distance smoke etched chimneys along a southbound road. Scobie was surprisingly cheerful. "We'll get there tonight, mate. 'Tisn't all that far, as the crow flies. You'll take to Doreen—she's all right."

Keith nodded, his limbs still numb. He was getting sick of Doreen—Scobie's big sister who sounded like a cross between Florence Nightingale and Joan of Arc.

5

Sprog had once been stolen out of a baby carriage. It was a long time ago, though, and he didn't remember anything about it—only what he had been told, mostly by the Foswicks. There had been a spell in a Home, before he went to live with the Foswicks. They lived in North London, and were the foster parents who, for a small charge, had taken him in after the Home closed down.

They had kept a small, crummy newsstand and had been too busy to bother with him very much. The elder Foswicks had left little impression on Sprog.

The one Sprog remembered was Bernie Foswick. Bernie was a lot older than Sprog and a whole lot bigger with it. Bernie had made Sprog's life a misery. From the start he'd made it clear that he wasn't having Sprog around longer than he could help, and that was okay with Sprog, too. When his tough little body had taken all the knuckle jabs it could, and when

Bernie's lies and tale-tellings had put him in so bad with the elder Foswicks that they thought they'd taken on a pint-sized monster, Sprog decided he'd had enough. He reckoned it would be years before he got big and strong enough to thrash Bernie effectively, and one night not so long ago he'd simply opened the back door and started walking. He hadn't bothered to think of things like stowing away food for a journey, spare clothing, or even where he was heading and in what sort of place he'd sleep nights. He'd just kept walking.

Unbelievable miles. Street after unfamiliar street, alleys into alleys, pavements unwinding like hard, gray ribbons; then country lanes and fields and woodlands smelling of wild flowers and wet with dew in the mornings.

He walked for weeks, sleeping where he could—telephone booths, barns, a heap of tarry coal sacks, the backs of parked trucks. When he was hungry he ate somehow—mostly by pilfering. Once or twice he begged at doors, but he got frightened when instead of bread he received curious stares. In the end even the kindliest of questions made him shake all over because he sensed that true answers would send him straight back to Bernie Foswick.

Sprog found it easier to steal: the odd bar of chocolate, a couple of apples from a fruit stall, a bottle of milk from a dark doorstep. He'd never been on the nick before, always understanding how wrong it was. But then, he'd never been that hungry.

It was a miracle that he wasn't picked up. Even the

busy, careless Foswicks must have reported him missing. Sprog never reached far out of London—the country oddly intimidated him and he kept feeling he was on a different planet. There had been one night in a barn, disturbed by a screech owl, and in the morning, very early, he'd screwed his eyes up in the sunshine steaming over a field of cabbages, tied a bit of string to his broken sandal, then headed back for the nearest chimneys.

By the time London embraced him again his gingery hair was a tangled mess and dirt had changed his complexion. He'd grown about an inch but had lost several ounces and now weighed a trifle over sixty-four pounds. His legs were stronger, the soles of his feet harder—though still sore with broken blisters. He had stolen and eaten a dozen apples, eleven bars of chocolate, six pork pies, eight fruit tarts, a couple of large unbuttered loaves, a bunch of unwashed carrots, six packets of crisps, some tomatoes and innumerable biscuits. He'd started out with five pence, but had bought an ice cream with that, way back.

Even Sprog would have admitted that he stank. There was not much he could do about his filthy clothes. Eventually he peeled off the remains of his socks and threw them into a litter bin. At that point he felt a little like diving in after them.

In London there is a lot of North. Sprog was careful to avoid his old familiar surroundings. Occasionally he'd hear footsteps behind him and have a vision of Bernie Foswick's burly, braggart, downright nasty presence bearing down upon him. Sprog reckoned it would take a lot of North London to swallow up Bernie.

East London was different and even by the bonfire Sprog had felt as far from Bernie as he might have felt in China. And in that basement where he'd followed the boy—he felt secure, warm, at home.

In a way, running off had been like unwinding a ball of string, looking for something new at the end. At the end was a knot, and the knot tied discovery and contentment together, with no thought of tomorrow.

6

The boy's match revealed very little before guttering out. A space—or a number of spaces partly separated by buttresses of brick and cement. Then the lamp was lit and a pallid light explored the depths, but the shadows from the buttresses and pillars robbed the place of any coherent shape and character. It was just a basement, entered through a door with a broken windowpane, and smelling of desertion and refuse.

One small part of it was different. A bay between two of the dividing walls had a swept, neat appearance. It was served by the kerosene lamp which the boy carried and hung on a nail above a bed of old blankets and sacks. Beside the bed was a small chest of drawers, and a rickety, basketwork table with strands of cane severed and hanging loose. There was a frayed, wine-colored rug by the blankets and a wooden box of the sort used to carry tools, on top of which ticked a loud, chipped alarm clock with a badly cracked glass.

"You *live* here?" asked Sprog.

The boy did not speak, didn't even nod. There was a slightly self-conscious, hesitant stance in the way in which he stood looking round, then patted the bed with the side of his foot and made a small adjustment of the lamp to make it less smoky. The dog lay down at once on some sacking apart from the bed, against the opposite buttress. The walls were quite bare, except for cobwebs.

"You want some pictures up there, mate," said Sprog, awkwardly. "Pop stars, or footballers. It won't take drawing pins, though, will it—that wall?"

Senseless prattle. With one who never answers, all conversation becomes senseless.

The boy showed Sprog the whites of his eyes. Somehow in the dim, friendly lamplight his face looked less strange. He picked up one of the old blankets and gave it to Sprog—not flinging it, exactly, but letting Sprog catch it across a foot or two of space, his attitude offhand, still only just short of hostile.

"Ta," said Sprog. "Mind if I borrow your washing line?"

There was a length of string tied to rusty nails above the lamp. Sprog took off all his clothes and hung them up to dry. Then he spread the blanket on the stone floor, and the sight and feel of it were as powerful as an anesthetic. He lay down just as he was, curled himself in it up to his nose, and was fast asleep in seconds.

When he awoke the window was gray but the basement itself held a darkness which seemed to belong to it. Somewhere not far off there was the drip, drip, drip of water. Above were faint footsteps and the sound of someone coughing. Traffic hummed in the distance.

Sprog yawned, wriggled, sat up and peered across at the boy's bed. It was vacant. The dog had gone, too. Sprog dressed, left the blanket in a heap and wandered stiffly to the door. There was the piece of glass missing at the top and the handle was tied with a piece of string to the remains of a latch hasp. The string could be reached with difficulty by shoving an arm through the broken pane.

Sprog came away and his foot caught in something and there was a sudden alarming jangle of cans. A trip wire of sorts. He'd missed it on the way across, and last night the boy must have led him clear of it. Sprog traced the course of the fine string a few inches above floor level. The end was tied to a hook in one of the buttresses and in between were empty cans strung along at intervals. Their jangle would give the boy an early warning of the approach of any intruder.

Against the opposite wall was a staircase with a broken banister. Sprog was halfway up it in curiosity when he realized, first, that it didn't seem to lead anywhere, only to what looked like an unbroken area of the floor joists above, and second, that if it did have a

40

destination, Sprog didn't belong there. Who could tell who lived in the house above, and what might happen to a head suddenly poking itself inquisitively through?

He came down again quickly and went to look for food. There was some stale bread in a box beside the boy's bed, and a couple of cans of beans. There was a little kettle, too, sitting beside a pile of ashes on two bricks. Sprog didn't fancy cookery, and he didn't want to nick the boy's food. It was early, and if he hurried he could find a milk cart somewhere not far away and steal a couple of bottles, maybe some eggs.

Sprog spat on his hands, smoothed down his hair a bit, and returned to the door. The surviving glass was thick with dust and anything moving beyond had a spectral, indefinite significance with a touch of menace about it; especially when it was accompanied by the oddest of noises. Louder than the dripping of water, yet of a not dissimilar metallic sound—like someone swatting flies on a steel drum.

Sprog moved so that he could see through the broken window. He could just make out a pair of immensely fat legs negotiating a mysterious descent into the basement area. A woman was coming down the metal stairs of a fire escape, feet in tattered slippers cautiously picking out the way. A huge aproned body followed the thick legs, then a large and florid face stared into Sprog's through the peephole.

The stare lasted a few seconds, then knuckles rapped unnecessarily on the window. Sprog, knowing that he'd been seen and having nowhere to run, opened the door. The woman held a tiny tray. On the tray was an egg cup, a boiled egg, two pieces of thickly buttered bread on a plate, a spoon, even a little salt on the edge of the plate. It seemed impossible, like a conjuring trick, that she should have carried it all down the fire escape from somewhere, guiding that enormous body down with one free hand.

"You're not *him*," she said indignantly. "Where's Charlie?"

"Eh?" said Sprog, startled.

The woman peered myopically at Sprog, as if still not quite sure. She smelled of gin and mothballs. Her hair was an unconvincing amber and her eyes were as shiny as two overfilled glasses.

"Charlie—that's what I call him. The one with the burned face. I brought his breakfast. You a chum of his?"

"Yeah—sort of." Sprog was looking longingly at the egg sitting temptingly in the egg cup.

"He wouldn't let you in otherwise," said the woman, already convinced. "He'd scare you off. All sorts try and get down there, you know. Tramps, people up to no good. Charlie scares them all off. Regular little scarecrow, he is, poor little scamp. What's *your* name?"

"Sprog."

"That's a queer name."

" 'Tisn't me real one."

"What is it?"

"I don't know."

Sprog didn't want to discuss his personal business.

"I'm just Sprog," he said with a shrug.

The woman was taken by his shrug and his pert, dirty, very hungry face. "*You* want some breakfast?"

"No, that's okay," lied Sprog.

The big red arms thrust the tray at him. "Oh, have it—I can fetch another. Where's Charlie gone?"

"I dunno."

"I hope he isn't out pilfering. I told him there was no need. He could come up and live with me, I said, as long as he wanted. There's only me on the second floor and Mr. Arthbut in the top floor back, except when my boy Max is home from his ship." Her eyes became briefly inquisitive. "Are *you* in trouble?"

"Not really."

"Going to stop here a bit, are you? *I* shan't let on, though others might, if you don't watch it. Mrs. Murgatroyd is my name. They're threatening to pull us down, you know. They've condemned the whole row. They'll have to get the troops out to shift me."

A black cat with a weepy eye nudged against her shin. Mrs. Murgatroyd gave it an affectionate, short-sighted look and said, "Eat your breakfast before it gets cold, then. I'll be back down with Charlie's breakfast. Let me have the tray back—don't drop the egg."

Sprog breakfasted contentedly. He'd learned to take people like Mrs. Murgatroyd for granted. People you met by accident dispensed kindness or indifference, or threatened you with the law, or tried to look after you as if you were a tame mouse. You took it all as it happened.

Sprog ate, hoping Mrs. Murgatroyd would bring

something to drink next time round. She'd have a job, though, balancing cups of tea on those stairs. Only it was getting a bit late for nicking milk. Sprog put the thought away, kept an ear cocked for a fresh sound in the area, an eye alert for the coming of a new shadow.

The dog arrived first, trying to push the basement door open with its paws. It didn't bark. A few seconds later the boy came in. He was carrying a bundle of clean-looking sacks. One of them, separate with the neck tucked under his arm, bulged a little.

He didn't look at Sprog. He dumped the sacks on Sprog's bit of blanket, then crossed over and did domestic things to his own corner, tidying the bed, sweeping up the ashes with an almost bristleless hand brush.

"I could have done that," said Sprog. "And ta for the sacks. I was going out presently to find things."

The boy emptied the separate sack. It contained firewood. He stacked it neatly into the wooden box beside his bed.

"Don't it get smoked out down here, when you light a fire?" Sprog asked. He persisted: "That old woman come down with your breakfast. She said I could have it. She's bringing some more, though. What's her name—Mrs. Mur-something?"

It had been a little trap. If the boy wasn't dumb, he should have come up with the name very quickly, unthinkingly. He didn't though.

When Mrs. Murgatroyd brought the second breakfast Sprog didn't interfere. He stayed on his own bed but he listened, hoping to hear some sort of conversation out in the area. But the interval between the two sets of metallic footsteps was short. The boy brought the tray back, and there was a chocolate biscuit for Sprog which he threw to him.

Sprog chatted on, avoiding questions, mostly just telling the boy things that had happened to him. Funny things, scary things . . . it didn't make any difference. The boy ate without answering or even showing that he was listening, and afterward he lay back on his bed with his head pillowed in his hands, the ghastly face softened by shadow, and in the end Sprog realized he was asleep.

So was the dog, stretched out as if dead on the bare floor with one eye glittering through a slit of eyelid. Sprog guessed, then, that they must both have been out much of the previous night.

Eventually Sprog dug a pair of badly worn sneakers out of his duffel bag and crept out. Suspicious, not of the boy but of possible marauders, he tucked his precious luggage under the sacks and picked his way through the basement door, up the steps of the area and beyond the broken railings into the street.

He stayed out and about all day. It was a day like many others, except that now he had somewhere to go to at night—a place he could retain in his mind's eye, curtained by events but always there, a place like a home.

He stole food and a new comic, but that was all. In

the afternoon a man gave him a job polishing cars at the back of a garage. He earned twenty pence and it felt like a fortune, honestly acquired.

When the evening closed in, with a mist creeping by in comforting wraiths, Sprog passed the shops where late lights glowed warmly—and he had twenty pence to spend.

He bought some chocolate, then next door he saw a hat. It was a knitted hat in the colors of a famous football team, and it had a pompon on the top and Sprog could see it on the boy's head, and he thought the boy might like it and it would be something to give him in repayment for the trouble he had gone to over the bed, his tacit friendliness in letting Sprog share his room.

It was hardly a thought, just an impulse, and Sprog bought it and was glad, for some reason, that he hadn't nicked it. When he reached the basement it was still half light. The boy was there with the dog. The boy had lit the lamp and was seated on his bed watching the basement door. When the cans didn't rattle he knew it was Sprog.

"Here you are." Sprog grinned. "Pretend it's your birthday." And he threw the paper bag, containing the hat, on the boy's bed. The boy undid the bag, saw the hat, and as soon as he put it on Sprog knew he was pleased.

7

Two days later, on Saturday afternoon, Keith and Scobie arrived by a second truck on the outskirts of the capital. Scobie reckoned you could travel for miles in London without even crossing a street. He had been trying to prove it for several hours, and Keith had the feeling they'd walked, run, climbed, stumbled and crawled in a gigantic circle. He was a mass of cuts and bruises and he had collected a lump on the back of his head from impact with the brickwork of a sewage dike. To make everything worse there were the first flecks of snow out of a leaden sky.

Scobie was talking less, which meant that he was feeling more sure of himself. There was a smug, cool look on his face, giving it an innocent, moonlike quality—the lack of expression an expression in itself. Scobie didn't feel pain much. A while ago he'd gashed his wrist on some rusty corrugated iron. He had sworn perfunctorily, sucked the wound till the bleeding stopped, then forgotten all about it.

At the high wall bounding a wrecked-car dump he said, "Give us a leg up, mate."

Keith let him plant his muddy shoes in his cupped hands and Scobie sat on the wall like a plump cat, listening, looking. Keith passed up the two pieces of luggage and Scobie threw them down on the far side. Then he gave Keith a hand.

It was another alley, on another cloudy night. Scobie's footsteps were quick and sure.

"You know where we are?" Keith asked.

"Of course," said Scobie. "This is home for me, don't forget."

Down an embankment they reached the towpath of a canal. Scobie stopped, sniffing, remembering. Keith picked splinters from his hands and gave his painful bump a tender stroke.

"Yeah," said Scobie, as if answering a question. "Come on."

Back to the streets, now, but in an area sparse of population and traffic. They still had glimpses of the canal between blocks of shabby buildings: warehouses, flats, factories, a large church with a thrusting beak-spire.

The street Scobie turned into was badly lit, close-packed with square tenements, heavy doors above railinged basements and broad stone steps. Many a window was boarded up. The street was short and narrow and it ended in a piece of waste ground surrounded by a timber fence. On the other side of the fence large machines waited with towering jibs higher than the church.

Scobie read the numbers, cursing because very few of the doors had numbers at all, and there were no gates. He had to do some simple arithmetic, working out from a ragged sequence which of the dwellings was Number Twelve.

"This is it," he said at last.

Keith was too tired to avoid a scathing comment. "I thought you said it was a hotel."

"What did you expect?" retorted Scobie. "The Ritz?"

Scobie raised a massive knocker. A light showed through garish colored glass. The door opened and a woman stood there, stared at Scobie with stupefaction, then grabbed him by the shoulder and pulled him inside. As an afterthought she didn't quite slam the door in Keith's face.

"I told you you weren't to come here. Didn't you get my letter?"

"No," said Scobie.

"Then some screw will have it. They'll know where you are."

"You think I'm stupid?"

"Who's he?" She gave Keith a contemptuous look.

"He's a mate of mine. He's okay."

"You can both scarper off. You think I want trouble?"

"Oh, come off it. . . ."

They argued on, Keith not listening, scarcely able to keep his eyes open. Eventually Doreen said, "I want you out sharp in the morning, see? If you're not, I'll put the police on to you, sister or not. You were always trouble, Scobie, and you always will be. And take those filthy shoes off, both of you. I suppose you didn't think to bring sleeping bags?"

So she wasn't quite going to chuck them back into the street. Though he was tired and on the fringe of Scobie's sullen duel with his sister, Keith picked up some undertones. Did Doreen have troubles, too? Her blowsy face was tight with anxiety, mascaraed eyes darting at the stairs, at the closed doors, at a pile of bags and suitcases in the hall.

"One night, do you hear? And you can sleep in the basement. I'll fetch some bedding."

She swung away, wide-hipped, high-heeled. When she had gone through one of the doors Scobie said, "She's all right, is Doreen. She don't mean nothing. She'll come round, you'll see." His manner was sheepish, as if he were suddenly ten years old. Doreen returned with a couple of shabby blankets. "You both need a bath. You haven't got lice?"

But she didn't offer the bath. From the hall floor she removed a stretch of frayed carpeting running alongside a cupboard under the stairs, rolling it up to reveal a square hatch with a sunken ring. "Give me a hand with this," she told Scobie.

They raised the hatch on squeaky hinges and a yawning chasm appeared.

"Down you go," said Doreen.

"What the heck . . . ?"

"It's the basement. It's perfectly dry. You'll be safe down there till morning."

"I'm not going down there!"

"What do you think it is—the black hole of Calcutta?"

"You could have fooled me!"

They stood there dithering, Scobie holding the blankets. Doreen said, "Listen, you roll up here uninvited and on the run. You expect feather beds and tea for two in the morning. You've got a choice, Scobie; and *you*, whatever your name is. You sleep in the basement or you beat it. It's all the same to me. Just make your minds up."

They groped in turn for the first step and Doreen went on, "I'll put the hatch down. You'll have enough light to manage—there's a window down there."

Keith heard Scobie's hollow feet run out of stairs, and his voice run out of soft curses. The hatch closed over their heads. Scobie had left his bag behind and Keith had to lug them both down, but Scobie had the blankets.

At the foot of the staircase Scobie said, "*What* light? It's as dark as hell down here. Get the flashlight out. Hurry it up." He sounded slightly scared. The flashlight was in Scobie's bag. Keith found it eventually and gave the switch a try. "The battery's just about had it."

"Oh, give it here."

Scobie swished the feeble beam to and fro, revealing nothing. He found a wall and flung the blankets down, kicking them into a flat shape. Keith could feel the anger mount inside Scobie—the anger and self-pity and enraged pain, like not knowing where to put a stung finger. He had a mental picture of Scobie hunched up in the back of the truck, just a few hours ago, alert, all wires, because of the new challenge, the fresh tilt against Authority. "Doreen mostly brought me up, see? She sort of . . . well, dotes on me, you could call it."

"And you wrote and said we were coming?"

"Of course. I told you."

"Yeah, but did you get an answer?"

"Not so far as I know. . . . You know what, Rabbit? You can be as dim as a ten-watt bulb at times. You think I was stopping back at the nick, waiting for the postman?"

Now, morose and full of a new hate, Scobie dragged at his bag to make a pillow.

"She couldn't even give us a room. I'll do for her, mate. Sister or not, I'll *do* for her. What's this place stink of?"

"I dunno," said Keith. "Rats, maybe."

"Rats!" said Scobie, making the word sound obscene. "We get out of one nick and here's a worse one—with rats for keepers. Let's get some shut-eye, somehow. First thing in the morning we'll scarper—but quick."

They both fell dead asleep without noticing the twin makeshift blanket beds in the next recess.

8

The boy and his crippled dog came and went. They came often while Sprog slept and they went, usually, when Sprog had just started a new conversation.

They suddenly upped and departed, yet again, late on Saturday evening, the boy having slept most of the day. He scarcely spared Sprog a glance, though he carefully put on the knitted hat before whistling for his dog and leaving through the basement door.

After they had gone the basement got creepy; snow began to fall past the window in the door, and Sprog went out. He made his own devious, discreet progress through alleys and yards—thinking over all that had happened, thinking of the boy. He remembered how scared he had felt, at first, of that sinister face, and of how in so short a time it had softened into familiarity. Even then, Sprog had found it hard to look directly at the boy. He'd known that the face couldn't hurt him, yet he'd chattered at the boy sideways, low down, looking at his own feet—anywhere but into those apologetic eyes sunk in ruined flesh.

Some day, when he looked back and remembered, it would strike Sprog that it hadn't actually *mattered*: the face wasn't the *boy*, only something individual about him, as freckles or ginger hair might have been, as were his gazelle walk and droop of shoulders and his wordless gratitude over the knitted cap. But now all Sprog knew was that he missed the boy and wished he wouldn't run off so often.

Then it suddenly hit Sprog that perhaps he had outstayed his welcome—if there had ever been a welcome. He made up his mind, there and then, that maybe he wouldn't trouble to find the basement again.

Then he remembered his duffel bag and knew that he'd have to go back. Later, sometime, he'd just call in and if the boy was there he'd say, "It's okay, I'm not stopping, mate. I've just called in for me bag." Then he'd leave, for good.

Not yet, though. What was the hurry? Sprog was hungry. He'd nick some food somewhere and find a new place to sleep, a place of his own. He rather fancied somewhere settled, sort of permanent, like the boy had. And if he found a place like that, *he* wouldn't want some other kid barging in either.

Sprog's nostrils picked up the scent of fish and chips. It came from a lighted shop along the street. His mouth watered. He went through the motions of searching his pockets for the ever-hopeful, forgotten coin, and as usual it wasn't there. There was no way of nicking from a fish and chip shop short of armed robbery, and Sprog had learned, the hard way, the folly of loitering about outside on the beg.

He turned his back on the light and ran down an alley—ran because the blast of wind cut through his clothing and a few flecks of fine snow touched his face like icy needles. A few moments later he knew he was heading for the basement. Just to fetch his bag, of course. There was a hunk of bread in it—and upstairs somewhere lived the fat woman who had given him breakfast. Sprog had just remembered her. "He could come and live with me if he liked," she had said, meaning the boy, not Sprog. But the sudden cold and hunger drove him into unlikely longings. And as his running warmed his blood, Sprog had second thoughts about the boy. Perhaps he hadn't actually wanted to be free of Sprog. Perhaps there was a different reason for his ins and outs at funny times.

Sprog stopped at a corner, dim with the feeble flicker from a faulty street lamp. A dog barked a sharp salute and there was the scamper of paws behind Sprog. *The* dog! Sprog tried to find the boy in the shadows but he couldn't see him.

The dog barked again, then slipped through a slit in a timber fence lining the pavement's edge. Sprog caught its bright eyes waiting and he crawled through after it. They were in a junkyard. The snow had stopped and the moon lighted the clouds and a small, bent shape scrabbled among the heaps, stacking occasional pickings into an old baby carriage. Presumably the carriage had also belonged to the scrap heap. Sprog didn't think the boy would have pinched it, throwing the baby out first. He glanced up as Sprog approached, then pushed the carriage a few bumpy feet along to a different heap and bent down again.

"Want a hand?" asked Sprog. He didn't expect an answer and he didn't get one—not even a gesture or a nod. He felt that the boy was needling him on purpose. He might be dumb but he wasn't stupid. "If you don't want me hanging around, mate, don't let your dog keep coming after me, see?"

The boy had come upon a small mattress in the heap. It had lain beneath a sheet of roofing iron, so it would be relatively dry, and it looked, at least by moonlight, respectably clean and not even very old. The boy *had* a mattress—Sprog had seen it under the sacks and blankets, yet he had troubled to pick up a second, which he threw over the front of the carriage, leaving a hole into which he could stack other things. The whites of his eyes sought Sprog's.

Other things came in pairs, or in duplicates of what the boy already possessed. Two pairs of rubber boots, a couple of extra plates, pots, pans, items of clothing. The carriage was soon as laden as a desert camel.

"Want me to help push?" asked Sprog.

The boy flung him a pair of sandals. "Ta," said Sprog. It made him remember the loss of one of his other pair in the canal. It all seemed long ago. He kicked off his tattered sneakers and tried the sandals on. "They fit, more or less! Ta." He squeezed the sneakers into his jeans pockets.

It was Sprog who came across the ancient phonograph. He tried out the handle, heard the hum of works; and there was a bundle of records, tied up with hairy string. The boy let Sprog pile the lot on the carriage. "I'll push, mate," he offered, and the boy let him, going ahead to open a gate.

They walked and bumped along the pavement, Sprog chattering. "I ought to know your name. If you can't talk, will you write it down—when we get home?" No response. "Mine's Sprog. It's not my real name. They used to call me Norman, at the Home—but they only made it up. I don't know my real name. I don't even know how old I am, neither. I was nicked out of a carriage when I was a baby."

Sprog had a feeling that the boy was listening. He went on: "They gave me birthdays, at the Home I went to. The first time they guessed I was eight. I shared a cake with a kid whose real birthday it was. They let me help blow out the candles."

Sprog had half forgotten where he was going. At an alley opening the boy grasped the carriage handles and gave them a twist. Then he let Sprog go on pushing. Sprog's voice sounded louder against close, brick walls. "Later on I was fostered out. . . ." Sprog told the boy about Bernie Foswick. Other people to whom Sprog had told his story had been horrified on Sprog's behalf over Bernie, but the boy simply loped on after his crippled dog, not even looking back.

"That's right, mate," Sprog bawled in pique. "Leave me to push your stinking load for you." He'd forgotten that the phonograph and records comprised most of its weight.

The boy came back and took half the carriage handle and helped push. Sprog said, "I could use some breakfast. Eggs and bacon, and porridge, and cereal and cream, *and* toast and marmalade."

They jointly bumped the laden carriage down the basement steps. The dog struggled up through the hole in the window. The boy went ahead and Sprog shoved the carriage under the fire-escape stairs. Inside the basement the oil lamp glowed.

Sprog went in after the boy. He was standing in his shrunken, frightened way staring at sleeping mounds of blanket in the brick recess next to theirs. Sprog was sure the eyes of a sleeper flicked open, stared back, closed again. The boy was off, lamp extinguished and abandoned, loaded carriage forgotten under the fire escape. Sprog's feet flapped after him up the steps and along the deserted pavement.

He soon thought he had lost the boy once more, but again it was the dog that betrayed his presence. He was high up on an immense timber stack behind a yard gate a couple of streets away. Sprog saw the boy climbing. He made his way to the timber stack and climbed too—hand over hand on the jutting timber ends.

It seemed a crazy place to have made for, until Sprog realized that it had not been at random. Along a timber tunnel, dark and resinous, there was a place like a tree house built of rough, left-over plank ends. There was a bed of sacks there and the dog settled down on them at once. As Sprog caught up, his knees rocking gently on the planks, the boy slumped cross-legged in his nest and his head nodded.

Nodded fast asleep, Sprog realized. Just like that!

"Poor little bastard!" murmured Sprog. "Why was you so scared, mate?" The dog placed its chin on stretched forepaws and wagged its tail. "They was only a couple of kids. Asleep, too. We could have bashed hell out of them, if they'd asked for it. It's *our* territory, not theirs. Tomorrow morning we're going back."

A few moments later Sprog was asleep, too, curled up between dog and boy.

9

It was the cold that woke Keith finally, so that he thought this was a first awakening and that everything else had been dreams. He lay on a floor as hard as ice with a draft from the broken window wafting in the stench of garbage.

It was early daylight. Scobie had flung the blankets down in what was little larger than a cubicle between two buttresses and all Keith could see was the short brick wall close to his feet and a shaft of gray beyond.

Keith lay thinking for a few minutes, flexing his stiff limbs, and when he found Scobie's red-rimmed eyes on him he said, "There was another kid in here during the night. Maybe two."

"What do you mean—maybe two? Can't you count?"

"One held a lamp. His face . . . ."

"What about his face?"

"I can't remember."

"Bet you was dreaming, mate. It wasn't all the supper we ate, was it?" He added, with the shock of recollection: "Rotten Doreen!"

There were gusts of rain across the dim window. Scobie closed his eyes again, his white face shiny and impassive, though his eyelids quivered—Scobie brooding, then wriggling in discomfort. Suddenly he sat up and said, "I bet there isn't even anywhere to wee down here."

He wasn't going out into the rain. He found a dark corner somewhere out of Keith's view, and his footsteps stopped abruptly on the way back, behind the buttress wall where they had their bed. "Come and have a shufty."

Keith went round. He'd been right, then—about the kids he'd seen. He saw the two makeshift beds, the bits of furniture, the bundles which Scobie had dragged from beneath the sacks and blankets. Then he spotted the trip wire alarm. Keith said, "They must be living down here."

"They don't no more," said Scobie.

He gave the little chest of drawers a swipe with his foot, spilling out drawers and contents. Then he picked up all the bedding in a massive bundle, carted it across to the basement door, kicked it open, and flung everything outside. He came back and ripped the trip wire from its hook and pushed the rattling thing into a corner. "The lamp'll be handy," he said. "Hey, let's turn out their bags." He flung Keith the duffel.

"You don't meddle with somebody else's gear," said Keith quietly.

"Give it here," said Scobie, snatching, ignoring the second bag. He used a pocketknife to slit the top of the duffel. Then he tipped it up. Out spilled a couple of brown apple cores, some tatty comics, a bit of chocolate in silver paper, a map, a little clothing, a bread roll with teeth marks and smears of rancid butter. "Big deal!"

He didn't bother to open the second bag but picked them both up, leaving the litter, and flung them through the door after the bedding. He gave the door a sour look. "If we can find a hammer and nails and some chunks of thick wood we'll board that up good and proper."

"What's the point," asked Keith, "if we're scarpering?"

"Who said we're scarpering?"

"You did, last night."

Scobie's eyes glazed then, and Keith felt the familiar crawling feeling down his spine like the drip of sweat.

"There are worse places than this, if we got organized."

"How do you mean, organized?"

"Oh, shut it!"

Scobie went back to bed, lit a cigarette, lay back under the clouds of smoke, noncommunicative.

Scobie *did* have a plan, then—something he'd thought out a long time ago. It hadn't been escape for escape's sake, and he'd probably not been surprised by Doreen's reception. He *wanted* to stay in the house, or under it if that was all he could manage. And whatever his scheme was Scobie would make Keith a part of it, leech on to him with sulky demands, drive them both to some point of no return. And Keith would feel sick and scared, but he'd go along because there was no way out.

The hatch opened with an abrupt clatter and Doreen came down the staircase with food on a tray. The crockery was old and cracked, as if she didn't expect to get it back. There were baked beans on toast and mugs of weak tea. Keith gulped his gratefully, letting Scobie do the grousing.

An argument developed and Keith watched them over his plate, in the spill of light from the hatch. "What do you think this is—a five-star hotel?"

"That's a laugh. You wouldn't get a mention in a book of dogs' homes."

"Little squirt. When you've eaten that you can hop it."

"You can't make me."

"We'll see, Scobie."

The threat sounded empty, though. She went up the stairs, last night's anxiety still in her eyes. Keith thought of the luggage in the hall, wondered if Scobie had noticed it and if he cared.

Scobie picked at his beans. Keith asked, "Do you reckon she knows about those other kids?"

"What other kids?" He'd genuinely forgotten. "Oh,

them. How should I know? I bet she never comes down here. We could nail that hatch up and all, then she couldn't."

They didn't talk for a while. At every slight sound Keith glanced across at the door, but the other kids did not return. Keith wondered if they were as small as Scobie seemed to have assumed when he'd chucked out their gear. At least if they turned out to be a couple of burly tearaways, Keith and Scobie would have the advantage of surprise. Only it might have been as well if Scobie had left the trip wire in position.

The rain eased off and Scobie said, "Let's go out."

"Where?"

"For a wash up, to start with. There's a gent's at the crossroads." He sensed Keith's hesitation. His eyes changed again. "There's nobody much about on Sundays. There's something I want to show you, too. A place . . . ."

"What place?"

"You'll see. Come on."

They went out into a street wet with the new rain; dingy, deserted, reassuring. Scobie had taught Keith nonchalance, a way of walking that attracted no attention. Scobie could do it even with his clothes caked with mud. Innocence was in his swagger, the way he held his head. If he'd met a policeman he'd have asked him the time, or the way to Sunday School, and got clean away with it.

Down the steps of the convenience a toothless, sleepy old attendant asked, "What you two been up to —having a mud bath?"

"Fishing," said Scobie.

"Come again?"

"Fell in the canal."

"You'll catch more than fish when you get 'ome!"

"Yeah," said Scobie. He paid for soap and towels —for two. Scobie always carried money. He knew when to nick and when not to nick.

When his hair was carefully combed and Keith waited patiently at the door of the cubicle, they went back up to the street and Scobie picked a route twisting in and out between tall buildings, mostly away from traffic ways. He came to a halt at the top of a wide driveway leading slightly downward toward a large flat building resembling a slightly down-at-heel aircraft hangar. A large sign along the front announced: STOCKPILE LTD.—WHOLESALE SUPPLIES.

"Some place, that," said Scobie.

Keith didn't answer—waiting.

"I used to work there."

"Yeah?"

"Before I was sent up. Only for a few weeks, though, but long enough."

"For what?"

"To know my way around," said Scobie. "A lot of pilfering went on in there and they hardly noticed. They've got enough stuff there to run a country. Food, tools, electrical gear—you name it. And you know what, Rabbit? I've got the open sesame!"

He must have been palming the keys for minutes, awaiting the chance to throw his little drama. There were two of them—Yales—on a slightly rusty ring.

"What are you thinking, Rabbit?" Scobie always knew.

Keith licked his lips: "It can't be—that easy."

"I never said it was *easy*," said Scobie with a rare grin. "The place is wired up like a bird cage and at night they have a dog patrol. But it helps having keys. We won't go hungry, mate. We won't go stinking hungry."

10

Music came faintly through the basement window—
a cracked tenor voice singing, slurred and wavery as
though driven by a slow, tired spring.

Scobie broke through the door, making as much
noise as he could for shock effects. The dog came at
him, barking and growling, and without giving it
more than a glance Scobie stuck out a foot and sent
the mongrel flying across the basement. It yelped,
then took refuge a safe distance away, yapping nervously.

The two smaller boys sat on bare mattresses with
sacks and blankets hung to dry near the oil lamp.

"Shut that mutt's mouth," said Scobie. "And turn
that ruddy row off, an' all."

The boy whistled and the dog went to him. Sprog
lifted the heavy pick-up from the record. In the silence Scobie's shoes squeaked slowly nearer the mattresses—that was for effect, too.

The two watching faces became clearer: one perky and freckly under a shock of curly hair like rusty wire, the other as brown and shriveled as a rotten apple. Scobie didn't look at it too long, but glanced at the freckly one.

"Beat it, titch," he said. "Pick up your junk and beat it. It's stopped raining now."

"Sprog," said Sprog. "Me name's Sprog. We was here first."

"Who's *he*?"

Sprog said, "I dunno. He can whistle, but he can't talk."

"What happened to his mush?"

"I don't know that, either, but you get used to it." He glanced at Keith in sudden appeal. "Look, mate, why should *we* scarper? We was here before you." He nodded toward the boy. "*He* found this place. It's his home, sort of, see? Was it you two who bunged our gear outside? It got wet."

Scobie scarcely moved, except for his arms. He reached down and lifted Sprog clean off the mattress. He held him by the shoulders and shook him till his short legs dangled like a rag doll's. Sprog knew a few tricks, though. He used his teeth, elbows and knees to half free himself. Sprog knew how to fight dirty, and when Scobie let go there was blood on his face. Scobie used his weight, then, smothering the smaller kid with his body and getting his hands at his throat. Then he sat up, used his knee to pin Sprog down and squeezed. Scobie's eyes had gone suddenly cold and strange and his giggle was more terrifying than a snarl. His big hands squeezed and Sprog's face changed color and his legs made desperate thrusts at the floor.

A couple of times at school Keith had heard the giggle and watched Scobie's whitening fists: some harmless tussles in the dormitory turning into out-bursts of savagery. He said, keeping his tone reason-able, pleading, very soft: "Don't kill him, mate. Look, you're *killing* him!"

Scobie let go then. Sprog staggered to his feet, lurched across the basement retching and holding his throat, finally throwing himself down on his mattress, his shoulders heaving with stifled sobs.

"I never hurt him," said Scobie. "I never hurt him. He wants to watch his lip, though, cocky little bas-tard."

He made no further attempt to oust the younger boys—the thought might never have occurred to him. The glassy look came back and Keith knew that his thinking had gone underground.

Scobie went and lay on his bed, smoking, and Keith dozed on his. When he woke, Scobie was squatting on his blankets shredding a cigarette packet into bits and scattering them as if he were feeding invisible pigeons.

In the next recess Sprog and the boy were busy sorting out their belongings, a couple of young beav-ers recreating their den. The old phonograph played, very softly, very scratchily. Scobie got up and strolled round, then sat on the box by Sprog's bed. At first Sprog pretended he didn't see him.

Scobie said, "Listen, and this time you can cut the back talk."

"Okay," said Sprog. "I'm listening."

"Does anybody else know you're down here?"

Sprog glanced at the boy. "There's an old dame who lives up top. She brought us breakfast, down the fire escape. She thought there was only *him.*"

"If she comes again you don't tell her about Rabbit and me—right?"

"Right."

"I'm not asking where you're from, or what you've done," said Scobie. "That's your business."

"Yeah," said Sprog. "I'm not asking you, neither."

"I bet you're a right little operator."

"I've been around." Sprog shrugged.

"Have you two been on the nick around here?"

"Not much. We got all this from a junkyard."

"Food?"

"You must be joking. Just bits and pieces."

"What about washing and that?"

"Washing?"

"It's a way of getting the muck off your mush."

"You don't have to nick water. There's always the canal."

"But you haven't tried it yet?"

"I ain't fussy," said Sprog.

"Watch it, that's all," said Scobie. "We don't want you bringing the fuzz back here or we'll all be for it. We're going to get organized—you'd be surprised.

You do as you're told and keep your nose clean, and I'll see you're all right, okay?"

The morning dragged by. Doreen made no further contact. The boys' tiny stove ran out of fuel, there were fresh flakes of snow against the basement window, and the only way to keep from freezing was to crawl beneath blankets and sacks.

At about midday Scobie threw his blanket aside, put on his mac and, without a word, went through the basement door.

Sprog came round the recess wall to Keith's bed space. There was a short, bent cigarette-end in his fingers. "Got a light, mate?"

"Smoking stunts the growth," said Keith.

"Oh, give over." Keith struck a match. Sprog sucked on the cigarette and coughed. "Where's *he* gone?"

"To get some food, I guess."

"You reckon he'll nick enough for us all? If not, I ought to go and forage for me and him. He won't go out in daylight, if he can help it."

"Because of his face?"

"Partly, but. . .I dunno. At night he comes to life, like a cat."

"You ought to give him a name, instead of calling him *him*." Sprog sat at Keith's feet. "Yeah. The old gal upstairs calls him Charlie. He's fast asleep again, and his dog. I don't know the name of that, neither. It's funny, when you don't know names. They call you Rabbit, don't they?"

"Real name's Keith, but Rabbit will do."

"I don't know *my* name," began Sprog, eventually getting round to the story of the orphanage birthday cake. He told Keith a bit more about himself, then suddenly changed the subject.

"Your mate—what's he really like?" asked Sprog.

"How do you mean?"

"Thank gawd you got him off me when you did. What did he do, lose his temper?"

"He does sometimes," said Keith guardedly. "I don't reckon he'd really have hurt you."

Sprog laughed nervously and gave his neck a rub. "You could have fooled me, mate. I hope he comes back with fish and chips. Pretty sly, is he, on the nick?"

"Pretty," said Keith.

"I wasn't going quietly. . ." Sprog jerked his head at the recess wall. "*He's* got other places to hide out in, but not as good as this. It was nice weather when I skipped and I never really thought about the cold. I s'pose if it got too bad I'd have to give up. Only I don't know what I'd do about him. I've got to sort of look after him." He shivered. "I'm going back to bed. It's cold enough down here to freeze a penguin."

11

Scobie came back, his coat flecked with new snow. His pockets steamed with hot pies and chips. He also carried a rusty gallon can smelling of parrafin.

Sprog was all admiration. "Cor, you never nicked that lot?"

"Fetch your plates, if you want to do it the fancy way."

Sprog woke the boy. Keith removed the metal cowl of the lamp, got it going, put some baked beans in a can and stood it on the supporting brackets. The beans would taste of rust, but they'd be hot.

"I never thought of that," said Sprog.

Scobie drawled: "Rabbit's got brains, see? He's thoughtful, is Rabbit. Where we come from they used to call him Einstein."

It wasn't true, but even Scobie had to have his little joke.

The boy sat apart, feeding his dog scraps. Scobie shot him short, disgusted glances, and when the food was gone he got up without a word, went round to his own bed and crawled under the blanket.

Sprog carried rubbish out to the area. When he came back he said, "It's snowing like 'ell out there. Freezing an' all." He crouched by the lamp, watching Keith replace the cowl and glass, warming his small hands by the smoky flame. "Him and me'll take another look in the junkyard tomorrow and see if we can find something bigger."

Keith went to his bed. Scobie leaned with his arms behind his neck, blanket up to his chin, eyes enigmatically on Keith. Next door the phonograph started up, a slurring waltz tune.

Scobie said, "Have you seen how he scratches hisself?"

"Who—Sprog?"

"No, the one with the face. Lice, I bet. We want to keep clear of him, mate. He's crawling. I've got news for you."

"What about?"

"Doreen." Scobie dropped his voice. "I come by a while ago and there was a car outside the front door. This bloke gets out, rings the bell and Doreen answers."

"Not the police!"

"She called him Howard. Who ever heard of a bogey called Howard? They all have names like Sid or Bert." Scobie's face was serious.

"Oh, come off it," said Keith.

"I haven't finished," went on Scobie. "There's a tatty old furniture van, too, just arrived."

"She's moving—already?" Keith thought it over. "That's why she hasn't bothered with us then."

"She can get lost," said Scobie, but Keith sensed that he was taking it hard. Perhaps he *had* nursed illusions about Doreen.

"Who was the bloke with the car then?"

"One of her crooked boyfriends, I expect. They'll be scarpering off somewhere, probably dodging the law. Suits me. Maybe we can move in on the floor above, eh? All modern conveniences. Water, gas, electricity—and that jazz."

"It'll be switched off, won't it?"

"It can be switched on again. There are ways, aren't there?"

"Yeah, I was only thinking . . . ."

"You think too much, Rabbit. That's always been your trouble. I'm off, soon."

"Where to?"

"I'm going to do Stockpile's tonight—solo, the first time." He thought about it. "Nothing to it. There's only old Peters and one mangy dog."

"Peters?"

"The watchman. He's still there—I checked him out. He's in his dotage, mate. Dotage! *And* he's got a wooden leg. He was at Stockpile's same time as me. Mean old codger."

Scobie glanced at his watch, waiting for the dark.

Mrs. Murgatroyd's cat wandered in, coat dappled with snow. It sniffed elegantly about, finally choosing Scobie's bedding to curl on and have a wash and brush-up.

Scobie shook it off. "I don't fancy cats. You know . . . I never fancied cats. They're sort of . . . in-human."

Soon after Scobie had gone, snow was shaken from the window and a flurry of movement ghosted through the iced glass. Someone tapped hard. Sprog got up. Mrs. Murgatroyd put her face to the hole and said, "Oh, it's you, sonny Jim. You've got my Charlie there, haven't you? Here, I brought you some extra blankets and a hot-water bottle. You can share it."

The boy didn't stir. Keith lay low. The dog wuffed at the window.

Mrs. Murgatroyd said, "She's moving out of the ground floor, did you know? Hussy! She never said she was going. Now there's only me and Mr. Arthbut at the top back. They're not going to get *us* out in a hurry, I can tell you. If you get too cold down here, you must come up along with me, you understand? You can trust me."

"Yeah, ta," said Sprog.

"With my poor old legs I think I'll move down to the ground floor, so long as those demolition men let us stay here at all. Nobody's to know the difference, are they? My Max is due home on shore leave tomorrow and he'll help me with my few bits and pieces. You won't let on, will you?"

"Not me," said Sprog.

Sprog came round the buttress wall to Keith. "Want a 'ot-water bottle?"

"What's the catch?" asked Keith.

"Nuffink. Only *he's* asleep and they give me chilblains."

"Chuck it here then."

Scobie was back in an hour, racketing about in the basement area, kicking snow off his shoes. He called Keith, who went across and pulled open the door.

"Help me cart this stuff through," Scobie said. He was breathless as though he had been running, but it was because of the load he'd carried. There were two large heavy round cans and a square carton as well as several smaller packages. They stacked the stuff on the floor between the beds.

"Easy," bragged Scobie. One of the cans contained seven pounds of baked beans, the other a similar quantity of stewed meat. There was a huge carton of assorted biscuits, packets of dried potato, crisps, sweets and cigarettes.

"Are we expecting a siege?" gasped Keith.

"Wholesale," said Scobie. "This is nothing, mate. If we got hold of a barrow we could get enough stuff to last for months. A van would be better. I can drive a van."

"*Months*?"

"You can get hold of just about everything in that place, not just fodder."

Sprog and the boy appeared, eyes ogling the food.

Keith opened the cans and got to work with his modified cooker; the light was dimmer but the air more fragrant. Sprog was full of admiration again, Scobie offhand but with occasional touches of bravado. The boy was silent and big-eyed, keeping slightly apart.

They ate all they could, fed the scraps to the dog and Mrs. Murgatroyd's cat, then Keith closed the lids of the two big cans and took them out into the snow, packing them in tight.

"Quite the little boy scout, aren't you, Rabbit?" said Scobie, and Sprog laughed. The boy crept back to his bed and Sprog went after him. Scobie kept the lamp.

That night they heard the last of Doreen. There were sounds from the floor above, the drag of furniture and the unsteady, heavy to and fro of footsteps; creaks of floorboards, doors opening and shutting, the rise and fall of unintelligible voices. Scobie lay awake, cigarette darting to and fro like a restless firefly. Doreen wasn't even coming to say good-by.

12

When the boy climbed out of his blankets, putting on his knitted hat and the boots he had picked up in the junkyard, Sprog was just drifting off to sleep. He thought for a moment that he wouldn't follow, pretending he was *really* asleep, but curiosity and habit roused him—also *he* had a pair of boots.

All the same this was one night, Sprog thought, when the boy might have stayed in. The basement was thick with kerosene fumes and the more acrid smell of Scobie's cigarettes, but it was several degrees above freezing point which was more than could be said of the streets above.

The steps up from the basement were as crisp as splintered glass. The boy did not wait for him at the top but vanished into the dark, white night, and Sprog yawned and half decided to go back to bed; but he hardly ever acted on half decisions.

It was at the first corner that the boy stopped and looked back: this is when he would have most missed Sprog had he not been there. He was a slender silhouette against the white-reflected light from a lamppost, a familiar shape, stance almost delicate as if etched in charcoal. In the night his face was blended with shadows, so that it no longer had to be taken into account.

"Where are we going?" called Sprog.

The dog seemed to be asking the same question for it padded on ahead, taking short, limping steps in the snow and just as short anxious glances backward. It was encouraging the boy toward the junkyard but the boy perversely swung right along a main street as deserted as a highway in Alaska.

The boy hesitated and with the barest suggestion of his eyes invited Sprog to follow. The dog limped after them into an alley lined with unexpected trees, a lamppost at the bend, the bend leading toward a closed iron gate.

The boy knew about the gate. He climbed easily over the five-foot wall beside it and after two faltering attempts the dog followed. Then Sprog. A freak, bright shaft of moonshine made hard shadows across a space marked by stones, turning it into moonscape. A cemetery . . . .

Sprog's chatter became subdued though as irrepressible as ever, words pursuing the boy the more incessantly because they never provoked a response. "Creepy, mate, that's what you are. What we looking at graves for? What's the point? We ought to have tied the dog up an' all . . . ."

It had sensed some living thing, gone darting into a maze of snowy pathways, out of sight—but it didn't make a sound. The cemetery was silent of dog's bark, of human voices, and only the low, steady wind played a faltering tune on the leaning stones and there was faint applause from overhanging trees.

There was a large grave marked by a rectangle of white marble, a tall, broad stone filled with names and words, beside which the boy stopped.

His lips moved, emitting no sound. He sobbed, but no tears touched his shrunken cheek. There was a series of sighs, breath drawn in staccato gasps—but no words.

Then the boy ran away. He ran in the direction his dog had taken, into the maze of stones. Sprog called after him several times, then he followed. He stopped a moment at the white marble rectangle. But unable to make out the inscription in the dark, he hurried on, in and out of the stones. But there was no boy, no dog, only the graves, stone after stone, and a long way through to the far wall.

"Hey, don't you go tearing off again," called Sprog. The boots felt as though they were made of lead, not rubber. The boy had vanished completely and Sprog had to follow the renewed barks of the dog. He shrugged his shoulders, used to this treatment, and with his usual optimism decided that a good run was a sure way of getting warm.

He ran on and on, following the barks. He arrived at a set of railings around a snow-coated square. It took him some time to find the gate, to discover without surprise that it was fastened with a padlock and chain—and he was not in the least astonished that the boy should have climbed clean over the top and that the dog had simply squeezed through an impossible four inches of railing gap.

Boy and dog waited on the other side. It wasn't until Sprog was over himself that he realized, with distaste, that they were in the playground of a school. At the top of some steps, close beside a row of snow-clad ashcans, Sprog hesitated, then asked in a loud whisper: "We're not going to *night* school?"

The dog knew more than Sprog: it knew that you could go down the steps and then, if you waited patiently, the boy would fiddle with the catch and open a heavy wooden door. As he did so, pushing the squeaking door inward, a wave of warm air was released—not too much of it because the boy held the door open only a few inches, and for only a few seconds. As soon as the dog and Sprog were inside he shut it casually yet quietly.

It was not quite dark inside. Beyond a soot-laden hinterland glowed a pair of immense boilers, roaring gently like captive lions. From each came an orange grin of fire beneath the flue shutters.

Their clothes were soon steaming comfortably. The boy sat hunched on an upturned box, warming his hands, behaving as though Sprog were not there, yet his arched figure was perhaps more at ease because Sprog was. Sprog chattered: "Cozy in here, isn't it? How did you come across it? What's to stop us making up beds and camping here for keeps? We could have buttered toast—if we had some bread, an' if we had some butter." Sprog laughed easily, unbuttoning his jacket to let more warmth in.

The dog went to the thick door and growled nervously. The eyes of the boy suddenly turned toward Sprog. It was the only warning the boy had time to give. Muffled footsteps were approaching the door, across the playground, changing rhythm down the steps. There was the sound of boots being kicked against the cement steps, then the rattle of the door latch.

The boy got behind the door, crouching low, holding his dog. The door opened with a blast of icy wind. Sprog, miles too late, backed toward the twin boilers, blinded by a powerful light beam.

"What are you doing in here, sonny?"

"Getting warm," said Sprog. Long experience of being detected in unlikely places had taught him the value of instant honesty.

"We aren't doing no harm—just getting warm," he added.

"*We?*" said the voice. All Sprog could see was a menacingly large shadow, but his worst suspicions told him that there was a policeman's cap at the top.

"We was only getting warm," repeated Sprog.

"Who?"

"Him and me," and it was too late to bite back the words. Boy and dog had made their escape, presumably darting from behind the opened door.

The flashlight flicked vaguely back at the door which had swung closed, a little mysteriously to say the least. "There were two of you then?"

There was no point in denying it now. "We been to cub scouts," said Sprog.

"On Sunday? A bit late getting home, weren't you?"

"Yeah," agreed Sprog.

"Where's your uniform?"

"Haven't got one, yet. I just joined."

"What about your mate?"

"Didn't you see his cap?"

"You're pretty smart with your answers," said the policeman. He sounded young. "This is a school."

"I know," said Sprog.

"The one you come to?"

"Yeah. The caretaker doesn't mind us coming here for a warm."

"At this time on a Sunday night?" People who talked to Sprog found themselves trapped into conversations they had no intention of beginning. "You're trespassing, you know."

"Am I?" said Sprog. "Sorry."

"I shall want your name and address."

"Sprog," said Sprog.

"Come again?"

Sprog chose the right moment to dodge sideways,

seize the door handle and take the steps two or three at a time. A boy like Sprog had no need to hit a copper. All he had to do was run and hide his identity in the night, and a falcon would have found itself at a disadvantage.

The boy, however, had an edge on Sprog. He made Sprog feel like a snail. In the lamp-lit street Sprog looked with hopeless admiration in all directions. "Lousy traitor!" he said, meaning the boy. "Lousy mutt," he added, meaning the dog.

Then he hunched his shoulders and headed for the timber stack, if he could find it, making a wide detour to avoid the police car squatting at the end of the street.

13

There was a short, rapid thaw next morning and fog which curled menacingly around the broken window of the basement. Scobie woke morose and silent, avoided looking at Keith, grabbed his threadbare towel and stumped up the staircase to the hatch, which he pushed open and allowed to thump shut behind him. There was the distant sound of running water, the flush of a toilet, and then footsteps wandering about on the floor above, hollow sounding in the deserted rooms. Scobie was making a lone reconnaissance, Keith supposed.

Keith got dressed. The younger boys had not come back. He had an impulse to go out himself, before Scobie came down. In the end he got the lamp working as a stove and spooned beans and potato into the rusty can.

Scobie came back. He muttered a "ta" when Keith

handed him a plate of food, then picked it over in a thoughtful way looking for burned bits which he flicked out with his finger and thumb.

"Them kids still on the loose, ah?" he said. "I'd like to know where they go and what they're up to. Say, Rabbit, you're handy with electrics, aren't you?"

"I learned a bit up at the nick," said Keith. "Why?"

"The current's still on upstairs. How do you reckon we could tap some of it?"

"Run a wire down—from a point?"

Scobie nodded. Keith told him about Mrs. Murgatroyd's plans to move down from the upper floor and Scobie said, "We'll have to be crafty, then, eh? And quick, too. Let's both take a look around."

Doreen had left nothing behind except rubbish: newspapers, bits of rotten linoleum, a few broken fittings. Her departure had been hurried and nobody had bothered to sweep up.

Scobie was right. No one had gone to the trouble to shut off the supplies either. Keith turned on a tap in the kitchen and doused his face. A hiss came from the gas tap he twisted. The electric light bulbs had all been removed save the one in the hall, but a light came on in there—presumably the fixture had been too high up to bother with.

"Mean old cow," muttered Scobie irrelevantly. It came out like a bitter, resentful epitaph, and he never mentioned Doreen again.

The cupboard under the stairs housed a coin slot meter for the electric supply and a point was attached to the wall, low down, just inside the cupboard door. Keith studied it, then explained to Scobie what they would need and how it could be rigged.

They replaced the hatch and went down to the basement. The kids' beds were like forsaken graves. Scobie kicked vaguely at the boy's mattress and the little rucksack he'd left at the head toppled over. Scobie eyed it with his usual mixture of curiosity and disgust, then went back to bed leaving Keith to clear up.

"Two sets of small footprints and a dog's paws," said the young constable. It was more like a confession than a report.

"A right mess you made of that, Two-five-nine," the sergeant remarked.

"They were only kids." Police Constable Jones shrugged.

"You didn't get the child's name then?"

"It sounded like Smog," said the constable.

"It sounded like Smog! And you didn't actually see a second boy?"

"Not actually, Sergeant, no."

"So what makes you so sure there *was* one?"

"I half saw him," said the constable.

"In transit, as it were."

"There were the footprints," said the constable. "In the snow. And the paw marks of a dog."

"No fingerprints?" The sergeant smirked. "Quite the little Sherlock Holmes, aren't you, Two-five-nine?"

"No, Sergeant."

"Now look here, Two-five-nine. The Divisional Inspector is getting worried about all the pilfering going on in his manor these days. It's most likely kids' work, he thinks, and so do I. Those kids, for all we know."

"Yes, Sergeant."

"The D.I. likes to think of his manor as a garden. You fellows out on the beat have the job of keeping it tidy. A little raking over, a little weeding—that's your job."

"I see, Sergeant."

"And you didn't do very well last night, did you, Two-five-nine? You raked over a patch of ground, that school basement where you took a look in, but you failed to root out the weeds, didn't you?"

"They was so quick, Sergeant," complained Private Constable Jones.

"You have a cruiser, haven't you, Two-five-nine? And we must get our trowels in and *root*, not come cap in hand with our excuses."

"No, Sergeant."

"Go to it, then, Two-five-nine."

14

It was after midnight. Fog lingered over the slush and the only sounds came from overfilled drains. Scobie paused on the edge of a driveway. Ahead, the iron gates of Stockpile Ltd. were padlocked. A seven-foot brick wall divided the drive in from a vacant lot. Scobie clambered up and gazed in the direction of a low building. It had a mortuary appearance with wired-over slit windows, and wide sliding doors closed and secured.

Scobie dropped down on the other side and crossed the vacant lot, leaving Keith to follow. An abandoned workmen's shed stood amid a litter of broken crates and other rubbish. Scobie had already picked the lock.

It was empty except for a few bits of building yard equipment. The window was of frosted glass, badly cracked. Scobie leaned cross-legged against a wheel-barrow and lit a cigarette. "We'll use this as a cache, see? We can lift the stuff over the wall and stow it here in one big haul at a time, then cart it in easy installments back to the basement. This old barrow will come in handy. I *have* greased it, so it won't squeak." Scobie had it all worked out. "Just follow after, and do everything I say, right?"

He squeezed the glowing end of his cigarette and put the stump carefully into his pocket. Then he eased the door open, took a cautious look outside and waited for Keith to come through. He worked his way along until he reached a pile of wood making rough steps halfway up the wall—Scobie had fixed those, too—and when they dropped down again they were on the drive inside the padlocked gates.

In the deep silence they could hear the low throb of a refrigeration plant. Scobie stopped and felt for his keys. Their eyes met, and Keith sensed Scobie's mockery. Scobie said, "You can stop out here if you want."

"What's the difference?"

"Your teeth are clacking, mate."

"They damn well aren't!"

"It's easy, we're not busting in, see? I've got one key to a side door the office staff use, and one from a passage into the main store. We don't set alarm bells clanging and old Peters and his mutt are patrolling the big truck park at the back, if they're awake, which I doubt."

"How do you know?"

"I've cased the joint, haven't I?"

The two doors opened smoothly and Scobie closed

them gently behind them and flicked up the safety catches in case, by some remote chance, anybody else should try to let themselves in. Faint light leaked through the glass roof. The wholesale store loomed over their heads. Long avenues passed between wooden racks laden with goods of all kinds: canned food, cartons, large quantities of kitchenware, clothing, tools, electrical equipment stacked on the orderly shelves as high as the roofing girders.

Scobie stood for a moment, directing a thin flashlight beam on it all. "They don't *miss* things, see? At stock-taking times they was always low on some stuff—maybe they blamed it on mice! We go careful, we don't get too greedy and we watch out things don't get spilt, leaving traces. Let's get moving."

Scobie used a ladder on wheels to fetch down several enormous cans which he handed to Keith, then cartons of crisps, sweets, biscuits, cigarettes and a couple of crates of beer.

Keith stayed in charge of a growing pyramid of supplies by the exit door. From the next row of racks Scobie brought a small electric heater and a huge reel of plastic-coated electric cord.

Keith said, "We ought to camp out in Piccadilly Circus."

"You always make cracks when you're scared, did you know?"

"I only meant, we didn't need so much wire."

"No? Well, I'm not wasting time cutting it, mate. Is it the right sort for fixing up to that point?"

"Yes . . . we'll want adapters, plugs and some adhesive tape."

"Help yourself. It's all round the corner, in trays. Hurry it up—I'll be rounding up a few tools."

Keith got the things he wanted. They tossed the small articles into a cardboard box. "Okay, that's the lot—for now," Scobie said. "About three trips to the shed should do it. I'll leave the doors ajar. Take it easy, see? No running, no looking suspicious."

It had *seemed* easy because Scobie was in charge. Scobie stole with the almost graceful nonchalance with which other boys rode bicycles. Even the fog was so convenient that Scobie might have provided it for the occasion.

They made three journeys back to the basement, using the wheelbarrow. By then it was first light and the kids were back, Sprog doing domestic things to his corner while the boy poured milk into two cups.

"Where did you get the milk?" asked Scobie.

"Where do you think—off a stupid cow?"

"Watch it," said Scobie. "Them milkmen are alive to that caper. You're to leave this stuff alone till we get back."

The dog was curled up asleep beside Mrs. Murgatroyd's cat. Scobie helped Keith to wire up the new equipment. Scobie put a couple of coins into the meter high up in the landing cupboard. It was a couple of hours before they had brought the cable down through a discreet hole bored into the floor, looping the wire along the basement joists and connecting it to a point screwed into a piece of wood fixed against the buttress wall. When Keith plugged in the heater and switched on, it glowed, throwing off an undreamed of warmth.

Scobie took off his shoes and watched his toes steam.

The younger boys crept nearer. Sprog's eyes widened. "Blimey! Where did you get all the juice?"

"We nicked a power station," drawled Scobie.

"Cor," said Sprog, impressed. "I must be dreaming." His eyes took in the fresh food supplies, the lamp with a luxurious satin shade and golden tassels. "You're a genius, mate." He meant Scobie.

Scobie basked in Sprog's adulation for a moment before grudgingly jerking his head at Keith. "*He* done it, all the technical side. He learnt electrics where we come from."

"Where was that?" asked Sprog.

"There was a screw called Tyson," went on Scobie evasively. "Him and Rabbit was buddies, sort of." The laugh was short and derisive. "That's the end of the quiz, Sprog."

"Yeah," agreed Sprog. "I wasn't being nosy. You got to learn though."

"Learn what?"

"How to get around, like you do."

"Just keep your eyes peeled then, and listen to your elders and betters. Reckon it's breakfast time, Rabbit."

Keith got on with it, knowing that Scobie was playing big for Sprog's benefit. Scobie and Sprog were swapping stories, Scobie patronizing but chummy, Sprog cross-legged on his bed, face earnest and watchful on Scobie. The boy sat glumly apart, nudging the dog's nose.

After the meal they were all exhausted. Keith tried to ignore the sounds of morning and fall asleep, half suffocated by the warmth building up from the heater. He glanced sleepily across at Scobie, saw that he was lying on his back toying with something in his hands. It was a knife drawn from a leather sheath, flashing with the reflection of the glowing heater.

Where had Scobie got a knife? He hadn't shown it to Keith, but Keith had seen something like it in Scobie's hand once before, during one of those fights in the dorm at school. It was the night a kid called Burridge had got out of his depth and "mixed it" with Scobie, finishing up squirming on the floor with the wicked blade an inch from his throat and Scobie's eyes like a reptile's.

Keith had said quietly: "Give us the knife, Scobie," and Scobie had handed it over at once. It was the night Rabbit learned of the power he had over Scobie and the night Scobie began to suck him dry with a thing called friendship.

15

On Wednesday afternoon Mrs. Murgatroyd said to her son Max, "There's something wrong with the electricity meter on this floor."

"How do you mean, Ma?" The previous evening he had carried his mother's few sticks of furniture down from upstairs. "It *gobbles* shillings," complained Mrs. Murgatroyd. "I've run right out."

"Here's a couple to be going on with," said Max, producing them from his pocket.

"I'll have to get the man in from the Electricity Board."

"Leave it to me, Ma," said Max hastily. "We don't want interfering busybodies round here."

Max disliked visitors to the house. In any case, he was always inclined to be touchy after one of his voyages. His face bore such an unhealthy pallor, too. That, as Max had explained, was because he was a stoker; not for him the briny breezes enjoyed by Jolly Jack Tars in the rigging. Besides, like Lord Nelson, he had never overcome a tendency to be seasick.

Mrs. Murgatroyd was always angry on her son's behalf, because his shipping line kept him so busy at sea—occasionally for a stretch of six months and, in these days when most ships ran on oil, *they* had found Max the last of the coal burners to stoke. No wonder he arrived home with such a haunted, pallid expression—as if he had been on one of the less successful voyages of Christopher Columbus.

Not that Max was poorly rewarded for his discomforts. And he seemed to spend very little of his stoker's pay, bringing it home all in convenient, well-worn pound notes stacked neatly in a false bottom of his seaman's holdall. As he said, "You can't trust nobody these days, Ma—not even your own shipmates."

Max was good to his mother and he regularly supplied her with bundles of the currency notes which, as he said, she ought to keep by her as a "little nest egg," apart from what she needed to spend. On the mantelpiece, next to the clock, was a rather large alabaster vase. Ali Baba himself might have raised his eyebrows had he peeped inside.

"I ought to put it into a bank, or the Post Office," Mrs. Murgatroyd had said once.

Max wouldn't hear of it. "Oh, you don't want to flash it, Ma. It's safe enough where it is."

On Wednesday, Max got on with his tea before

examining the meter. He always ate like a horse after a voyage.

Max said, "I suppose you'll be next out, Ma, now Doreen's gone."

"That hussy!" snapped Mrs. Murgatroyd. "I expect *she* tampered with the meter."

Max shook his head. "Reckon I'll have to find you a nice little place in the country."

"Oh! Cows and chickens aren't in my line, son."

"But they've condemned this house, haven't they?"

"They won't get *me* out till they push a bulldozer clean through the front door."

"That's the spirit, Ma." Max laughed. "You don't want nobody to shove you around, see?"

"And I wouldn't say I was lonely. There's me cat, and me parrot, and Mr. Arthbut you can talk to if you shout. And people I come across in the shops. And there's Charlie."

"Charlie?"

"You must promise not to get angry about Charlie," said Mrs. Murgatroyd.

She told Max about the boy who lived in the basement. She did not think it wise to mention the second one and so far she had not learned of the others.

Max asked: "What are you going to do with him?"

"You can't *do* things with him. He comes and goes. I feed him on occasion, but he seems to manage. I try to talk with him, but he can't talk back."

"Can't or won't?"

"He's perfectly honest," said Mrs. Murgatroyd.

"Has he got a certificate to prove it?" quipped Max. "He doesn't know what's in the you-know-what?"

He meant the alabaster vase. Mrs. Murgatroyd snorted. "Certainly not. He never comes much farther than the top of the fire escape. He's like a little mouse —out of a hole."

"What hole?" asked Max, his eyes thoughtful. "And had you reckoned on somebody looking for him —maybe even the police?"

"I suppose I *ought* to report him," said Max's mother. "I was meaning to, for his own good. I just haven't got around to remembering at the right moment."

"Do it anonymous," said Max. "You don't want the police round here asking a lot of questions."

"No," agreed Mrs. Murgatroyd. "He's all *right*, I think. Wherever he comes from, he'll go back when he fancies. He's like quicksilver. You should see him run!"

"I might at that," grunted Max darkly.

After tea Max Murgatroyd took a long, mildly perplexed look at the spinning wheels in the meter. To judge from their rate of progress Mrs. Murgatroyd, at that moment, was consuming enough electricity to floodlight a football stadium. Max's slightly hooded eyes dropped to the complex of wires sprouting below the box, threading through metal staples toward different parts of the house. All seemed in order there.

Max closed the door of the pantry with the toe of his shoe, then went through the floor room by room examining the points. In the hallway behind the frosted glass of the front door his feet squeaked on the hatch below the threadbare rug, but he didn't notice. There was an electric point not far from the door, but a substance like chewing gum had been wedged into the holes—presumably to cover some fairly dangerous defect. Max kicked the point gently and distastefully, continued with the disconcertingly light footfall he habitually adopted at work, checked every other point he could find, and only then did he return to the stair cupboard and spot what he'd previously overlooked.

Interesting! Hopefully concealed behind some dusty pickle jars was a point from which curled a shiny, black, newish length of plastic-covered cable. So far as Max could make out it was connected to no visible appliance, but snaked mysteriously through a hole in the floorboards—the sort of hole made long ago by some primeval mouse.

Most interesting. Max treated himself to a little smile. He felt a strong impulse to yank out the plug, but Max never performed a simple action when a more complicated one might prove more intriguing.

Somebody, somewhere, was illegally tapping the electricity supply. Max swore softly in indignation. Nobody put a caper like that across Max Murgatroyd and got away with it!

Max stroked his chin and crossed to the dusty kitchen window. Fog lay heavily over stale snow. It was impossible to make out such clues as footprints, or signs of entry and departure, through the weedy back-yard.

Max returned and gave the plug attachment a further, quizzical glare: a boy such as his mother had described had never worked that cunning little piece of gadgetry. He blew his nose, went into the living room where Mrs. Murgatroyd and her cat were watching TV, and said, "Not to worry, Ma. It's just a little technical hitch. I'll soon sort it out."

16

———

Scobie dragged Keith out twice on Wednesday night to help him rob Stockpile's. Keith, more scared each time they did it, couldn't see the point. The basement was already glutted with stuff they would never use.

On the second trip Sprog wanted to come too. At first Scobie wouldn't hear of it, but he gave in, finally. As far as Scobie ever took to anybody he had taken to Sprog.

"We won't get in the way, honest," Sprog assured him.

"*He's* not coming," said Scobie, glowering across at the boy.

"He won't get hisself nabbed. He can get in and out of windows like a cat."

"We're not going through any windows," said Scobie. "And we're not taking him. He's marked. I'm not saying he can help it, but he's marked. With a mush like that, if anybody spotted him they'd soon track him down, and we'd all be blown."

Sprog hesitated; it was about the time they both normally went out for the night. The boy's eyes did not meet Sprog's.

"Won't be long," said Sprog. "You wait for us, eh? You look after the gear. I'll bring you back something as a treat. Sweets—or something."

The figure looked gnomelike, the awful face pensive, profile blurred.

Outside a bitter wind murmured through the railings. Only Keith seemed to feel it. As there were three of them, Scobie said, they could skip using the workmen's shed as a cache.

Scobie used his keys and a flashlight. He stood inside the building hesitating, as if wondering what to steal next. "We could do with some more blankets," he said. "What else?"

Sprog was too overwhelmed to answer. "Cor," he said. "I never been anywhere like this before. How did you find it, Scobie?"

"I used to work here," said Scobie. "I took wax copies of the keys before I left. Nobody knows."

"That was smart."

"I'm not just a pretty face," said Scobie complacently. "You do what you're told while you're here."

"Sure," said Sprog.

He was all activity, the small boy wanting to explore. He got aboard one of the big trolleys and grabbed the steering bar. "Give us a push."

"Cut it out," said Scobie. "We're not here for the lark. You'll make a row."

"It's got rubber wheels. Give us a push."

Scobie was handing Keith blankets in plastic coverings. Sprog managed alone—thrusting the trolley along as if it were a giant scooter, pushing with one foot. The vehicle careered along the gangway and collided with a pile of cans, sending them scattering. Scobie swore at him. They all had to spend valuable minutes restacking them. Afterward Sprog vanished for a while and Scobie and Keith assembled some supplies which Scobie had decided they needed: the blankets, spare batteries for the flashlights, cans of beer, cigarettes, the biggest kettle Keith had ever seen, and a transistor radio.

"We need a camel," said Keith.

"Where the heck's Sprog?" asked Scobie.

High up on one of the giant racks! They didn't see him at first, but his husky whisper came down audibly enough from the heights. "Hey, the roof opens, just here."

Scobie picked him out then: a small, shadowy shape wriggling in his flashlight beam. "Come down," said Scobie angrily. "You'll set the alarm off."

"What alarm?"

"The roof's wired!"

"Not this bit isn't. I can see out on the roof. The fastening's busted."

"Come down!"

"Okay, I'm on me way."

Sprog clambered down the racks, tracked anxiously by Scobie's torch. He jumped the last six feet.

"See how much you can pick up," said Scobie. "We make a beeline for the basement."

As they went through the second door a dog barked and a flashlight beam struck them sideways. A man's voice said, "Hold it there!"

They scattered. Keith made for the nearest part of the wall and the dog was on him in a second, snapping at his feet. He sat on top of the wall trying to beat the dog off with his feet, but it kept coming. Keith was carrying a couple of cartons. He half dropped, half threw them, hoping they would find their target—and they did. The dog yelped. Keith dropped down on the other side and ran.

He ran, empty-handed, all the way to the basement. When he was sure he hadn't been followed he went down the steps. Somehow he had expected to arrive first but Scobie and Sprog were there ahead of him. There was no sign of the boy. The light had been switched off and before putting it on again Scobie used his flashlight to check that it was Keith who had arrived. He sighed with relief, then switched on the light.

"You weren't followed?"

"No."

"What happened to the stuff?"

"The dog was on me. I chucked the boxes at it."

"Oh, very clever."

"What would you have done?"

Scobie didn't answer that. He had brought his share back and so had Sprog. The plastic-covered blankets were on the floor.

"Who saw us?" asked Keith.

"Old Peters, the watchman," said Scobie.

"The game's up then."

"It's no game, mate," said Scobie.

"What else could I do?"

"I ain't complaining, am I? I'd like to know what brought the old geezer round. It's way off his pitch."

"If somebody saw the skylight shift . . . ."

"Don't go blaming Sprog," said Scobie, lighting a cigarette. "He's all right, is Sprog. Got the nerve too."

"I wasn't *blaming* him. . . ."

"I bet he never really saw us," said Scobie, ignoring Keith's denial. "He's as blind as a bat."

Sprog grinned at Keith. "Say, Rabbit, I'm glad you drew that mutt's fire. Dogs always make straight for me trousers. Anyway, them boxes only had pickles in them."

"I only hope they never had fingerprints an' all," said Scobie.

Sprog looked sharp. "I bet you *have* been in Borstal," he said, as if Scobie and Rabbit might once have played soccer for England and were too modest to admit it.

"One day," said Scobie, "I'm going to use your nose for an ashtray."

Sprog grinned, then looked more seriously across at the boy's deserted bed. "*He's* gone. I guessed he would. I ought to go and find him, really. I mean, every night lately we've been together, and he'll miss me around."

"Here's your new blanket," said Scobie.

"Yeah . . . ." Sprog looked tempted. "He's got his dog. His dog takes care of him, you know?"

Keith made cocoa. Scobie ignored it and gulped down two cans of beer. They delved deep into a new tin of biscuits.

Sprog said suddenly to Keith, "You talk a bit different, don't you? You use long words, sometimes."

"Do I?" said Keith. So far as he could remember he hadn't uttered a word except to ask Sprog how much sugar.

Scobie leered. "Rabbit was brought up different from the likes of us, see? He only ever went on the nick once, before we come here. For real, though. Fifty nicker *and* he half killed some old codger in lifting it."

A denial leaped to Keith's tongue but he bit it back.

Sprog looked at Keith curiously. "Go on." he said. He was about to ask more questions but he thought better of it.

He saw that the boy had left the knitted cap behind. It lay on the bed, abandoned. "He never took his hat," said Sprog. "His head'll get cold." He meant more than that.

"Want some more cocoa?" asked Keith.

"I could use a real drink," said Sprog, lifting the sentence straight out of TV.

107

"Here you are, then," said Scobie, flinging him a can. Sprog gulped the beer. "Shall I put the phonograph on?"

"That old stuff," said Scobie. "Cats on tin roofs. How's this for tone?" He switched on the transistor he'd stolen from Stockpile's and found a late foreign station playing pop music.

"That's what I call class," said Sprog.

The pair of them got through the crate of beer and it didn't take long. Scobie began to look wild and Sprog thought that every remark was the joke of the century.

The boy came in, his dog lingering behind him. Scobie froze. "Tell you something?" he slurred. "I've always wanted to know what *he* keeps stowed away in his little old bag."

"Eh?" said Sprog squiffily.

Scobie fixed blue eyes on the boy. "Come on, mate. Open up your gear. Let's see what you've got."

The boy grabbed his bag, hid it behind him, tried to draw into the shadows.

Keith said, "You're sloshed, Scobie. Leave the kid alone. What does his gear matter?"

"Shut it," said Scobie, and when Keith went for him he fought back. Keith couldn't hold him for long. When Scobie had him on his back, arms pinned beneath his knees, he suddenly knew that in more ways than one he had lost his hold on Scobie. It was over.

Then Scobie backed away and drew his knife.

The long blade twinkled and there was a pause while a love song whispered incongruously from the radio. The other boys crouched, waiting.

Scobie's eyes broke away first. With an almost casual flick of his arm he sent the knife hissing across the basement. It stuck, twanging faintly, in the joist immediately above the boy's head. Then, without a word, Scobie lay on his bed and rested his head in his linked hands.

Sprog grinned at Keith but didn't speak.

17

The Divisional Inspector's office upstairs at the police station, furnished with desk, chairs, filing cabinets and papers stuck on a notice board near the door, might otherwise have been mistaken for a small annex of Kew Gardens. A row of pots, touching almost rim to rim, occupied the broad window ledge overlooking the canal. A wide variety of plants stood on soil-smudged saucers and one, close to a radiator, even displayed an unlikely bloom of pale yellow petals.

Sergeant Len Bowers sniffed disapprovingly at an exotic foliage labeled with a wired tag bearing an incomprehensible Latin description. He opened an extra window surreptitiously and watched the billows of blue smoke curl out. In his opinion, Inspector Bainbridge would save himself a fortune if he threw out all those obscure Latin growths and planted tobacco instead.

Divisional Inspector Bainbridge prodded delicately

at one of his succulents with the tip of a ball-point pen. "Like an allotment in winter, Sergeant. Nothing much to do except rake in the frost for slugs."

The Sergeant said, "There's always Max the Sailor." He tapped his fingers on a report put in by an ambitious young detective constable to the effect that "an old friend" was in circulation again following a stretch in Parkhurst Prison.

"Potatoes," said the Inspector.

"Pardon, sir?"

"People like Max Murgatroyd are like potatoes. You think you've dug the whole lot up, but sure enough the following year there's one sprouting among the dahlias."

"He got six months last time."

"They should have made it six years! Soft judge on his case. He's gone home to his dear old mum, according to that report. Aren't those old tenements supposed to be condemned?"

"It would take a lot to condemn Mrs. Murgatroyd." The sergeant grinned. "The parrot probably bit the man from the Council. It bit me once."

Sergeant Bowers was remembering a visit he had made to the house long ago, pretending to be a shipmate of Max's, just so that he could ask some tactful questions.

"That bird could tell some tales," commented Inspector Bainbridge. "Maybe we'll pull it in before long. Meanwhile, keep all the lads turning their spades, Sergeant."

Weightier matters occupied the inspector for most

of the day and it was the sergeant who eventually interviewed a Mr. Peters.

"Used to be one of us," announced the station clerk. "Say half a century ago. Now calls himself a security guard at Stockpile Limited. He insists on seeing the Commissioner of Police, unless there's someone higher."

"He'll have me and like it." The sergeant sighed.

Young policemen always showed courtesy and kindness to old policemen. Sergeant Bowers took Mr. Peters into a spare charge room and ordered tea and biscuits. "D Division before the war," said the old man. "I was a sergeant, too, in the end."

Sergeant Bowers listened patiently for a few minutes. He felt like making sure the door of the charge room was kept closed in case the draft blew Mr. Peters away. He was the thinnest, whiskeriest old chap he had met in a month.

"That's not what I come about, though," said Mr. Peters, his watery eyes serious. "It was these kids, last night. I don't know whether they was trying to get in, or coming out. And I think I recognized one of 'em."

Sergeant Bowers asked a question or two before going on. "You've reported this to your employers?"

"Not yet."

"Why not?"

The old man looked uncomfortable. "I'm not sure of anything—not enough. If it was only kids larking about it's my job to keep them clear—mine and Prince's."

"Your dog?"

"That's him. What makes me think they must have got in, and out, is that I come across a couple of cartons of pickles near the wall. They *could* have fallen off a truck."

"Pickles! But you don't think so?"

"Not really."

Sergeant Bowers got the message. Mr. Peters, with his artificial leg and failing eyesight, held on to his job by a thread—a thread of somebody's sympathy or negligence. Stockpile's had a reputation for being cheap: they didn't think it worthwhile to spend large amounts on security arrangements.

"Tell me more about what happened last night."

"I could've been wrong. The doors hadn't been tampered with."

"Which doors?"

"Small ones at the back, which the office staff use. The locks weren't broken or nothing."

"So?"

"If they got in they must have had keys."

"I see. . . ."

"The lad I remembered used to work on Saturdays in the store a couple of years back. He got into trouble and they put him away."

"That should be easy enough to check," said Sergeant Bowers. "What was his name?"

"I dunno. Everybody called him . . . Toby, or some name like that."

"Scobie?" asked the sergeant sharply.

"Yeah, that'll be it. Scobie. A right tearaway he was, with cold eyes and enough nastiness in his nature to block up a drain. How did you know?"

The sergeant didn't tell. He turned sympathetic eyes on the old watchman.

"It'll be all right, Mr. Peters. Tell your employers what happened. You can fancy it up a bit if necessary —no need to give them the idea you weren't up to your job. We'll get in touch with them. All they need to do, by the sound of it, is change those locks."

18

Scobie took Sprog alone to Stockpile's on Thursday evening. Back at the basement the boy slept and Keith brooded in his corner—waiting, he wasn't sure for what.

They were gone less than an hour. Sprog wasn't quite his perky self and Scobie looked thunderous, flinging himself straight onto his bed and biting his thumb.

At first neither of them brought Keith into their conversation. Sprog toasted himself by the fire and said, "I could have done it—easy."

"I wasn't chancing it," said Scobie.

"The top of that wall, then up a drainpipe, across the roof . . . ."

"You'd have slipped off, making a row—if you didn't break your neck."

"Easy," insisted Sprog. "A carthorse could have done it."

"Oh, give it a rest," said Scobie. Then he unsheathed his knife and practiced sticking it into joists. He soon got tired of that and, with no change of expression, aimed the blade at Sprog's head. Sprog grinned nervously.

"What happened?" asked Keith.

Scobie, eyelashes white in the electric lamp, said sulkily, "They've changed the locks."

"At Stockpile's?"

"No, Buckingham Palace." Scobie's sarcastic snarl was a part of his new, contemptuous disregard of Keith. He went on: "They must have guessed. I suppose they *must* have. Old Peters must, and reported us." Suddenly Scobie was a small boy explaining how the farmer had spotted him stealing apples.

"I wanted to climb through the skylight," said Sprog, half to Keith, the other half reproaching Scobie. "I wouldn't have fallen or nothing. If the other night I could poke me head through from inside, what was to stop me climbing through from outside, on to them racks?"

"Blow your nose and shut up," said Scobie.

"We could have got the stuff out the door just the same, because you only have to turn the knobs inside. You want to bet?"

"I'll think about it," said Scobie, peering at his knife, tipping it gently from side to side and watching the reflections on the joists. "Anyway, old Peters and his mutt were practically breathing down our necks. They must have been warned."

He went to sleep soon afterward. Sprog went to bed too, glancing at the sleeping boy. After a while, soft as a cat, the boy crept out—alone. He didn't take his dog this time. It followed, a little late, and found the door shut against it. It stood there, tail drooping, whining for a moment; then it gave up, sniffed round the basement, and lay down on its sacks. Nobody had switched the lamp off so Keith yanked out the plug, leaving the heat glowing on one rod. For all the gadgetry, the basement did not seem to have lost its gravelike atmosphere; stale food merely added to the familiar putrefaction.

Keith lay thinking for a long time, waiting for Scobie to wrestle with his first nightmare. Later he'd wake up as bright as morning, if he got into that sort of mood, switch on his radio, twiddle about between foreign pop stations and the local police. The night would be punctuated with his restless movements.

Somewhere, away from the house, a hammer tapped urgently and fussily, like a woodpecker pecking in a hurry. The senior magistrate had rapped like that with a pencil. "It is not often that we have the painful duty of presiding over a case as distressing as this. . . ." An elderly, birdlike, rather shocked sort of person hunched in an oversized chair, twiddling with a tiny pair of gold glasses. Williams, Bryson, French and their parents. And Keith's mother, sitting apart. Sunlight twinkling through the dust, furniture polish, the smell of old books. No Turner though. Turner was lying low—artful, gloating and guilty. The small indignant eyes swiveled on Keith. "In your case, young man, we were unable to agree that a period of probations would be a suitable expedient. . . ." Only for Williams, Bryson and French.

Keith knew that he'd made up his mind. That is, he had the *answer*: there remained only the *questions*. How could he get back to Darlington? And if he didn't, if he simply walked out and presented himself at a police station, would he be nimble enough with his replies? "Where have you been hiding all this time? Demolished house—which demolished house? Junkyard—*which* junkyard? Who were you with? Nobody? Come off it, son, you didn't do all this on your tod! What became of that other lad you were with—Scobie? Where is *he*? You don't expect us to believe that you split up in Birmingham? Suppose I was to tell you that someone *saw* Scobie?

They'd get it out of him about Scobie. And some day Scobie would be back at the School, too, and try telling Scobie you hadn't grassed on him! Yet it was more than that.

There was another alternative; grab his belongings, *now*, open the basement door, go quietly up the area steps. Break away, take his chance. . . . What chance, though? A boy in an unfamiliar concrete jungle with no contacts, no means even of keeping alive except by reckless, incompetent pilfering. He'd be picked up in hours. That would be worse, *look* worse —if he was caught instead of giving himself up.

Suddenly Keith thought of Scobie's knife, and he

felt cold. He could make out Scobie's white face, the hillock of blanket his knees made, and the old sense of pity and responsibility came back to him, as if in Scobie he had found an ill-matched brother.

Keith wanted—as perhaps he'd always wanted—to *hate* Scobie, as he hated Turner; Turner with his leering deceit and fat lips and pink bubble of chewing gum which he'd burst obscenely in your face. At the school, Turner had provided Keith with illusions of tomorrow; Keith had sent himself to sleep, night after night, with wild plans of pursuit and revenge. But now the face wouldn't come to mind, only Scobie's, and Keith had nothing to latch his hate to, and tomorrow was full of questions.

Tomorrow, should he give himself up and "shop" Scobie too? Because of the knife? For the sake of hero-worshiping Sprog? Because he, Keith Burrows, got windy every time he saw a policeman's helmet? For his mother's sake? Or on account of Tyson's betrayed trust?

Too many questions; too many answers. . . .

"He's come up," said Mrs. Murgatroyd.

"Who's come up where?" asked Max.

"Charlie. He came to the kitchen upstairs, of course. He didn't realize we'd moved. You mustn't be cross."

"Ma, you've got me all wrong. Why should I care about a kid?"

"Well, you said . . . . Anyhow, when he's finished his supper I'll pack him off."

"Back to the basement?"

"I suppose so."

"Let me have a word in his ear."

"It won't get you far. He doesn't talk."

"I'm good with kids," said Max.

"What is it you want him to do?"

"Nothing," lied Max. "I'm just curious."

"About Charlie? Well, *he*'s a curiosity, I'll grant you that. Poor little scrap. He's still up in the first-floor kitchen."

He wasn't though. Max could walk as quietly as any man, but the boy had gone, leaving the fire-escape door slightly open so that a nasty draft cut across the empty room. Perhaps he had simply finished his supper or perhaps he had heard Max talking. Max studied the door. He looked down toward the dark back yard, then went downstairs.

Mrs. Murgatroyd said, "You won't catch him now. He'll be off, will Charlie."

"Where?"

"How should I know? He's in and out, as I told you. Like a jack-in-the-box."

"Or a mouse," said Max. "That's what you said at first, Ma. A mouse."

He'd wanted the kid to deliver a message downstairs, but never mind. There was more than one way to skin a cat!

19

At the police station, on Friday morning, Sergeant Bowers was called to interview another visitor who'd asked peremptorily for the Criminal Investigation Department. He turned out to be a shabby, shaggy young man with hang-dog jowels and the glitter of an idealist in his large, brown eyes. Leather patches were sewn into the elbows of an old tweed jacket, and the sergeant thought he had "schoolmaster" written all over him.

"Name, sir?"

"Walter Frank Tyson."

"Occupation?"

"I don't see . . . ."

"Just for the record, sir."

"I'm an electrical engineering instructor at an Approved School."

"Name of school?"

"This is really an informal inquiry. Actually I'm on leave."

"Not very good weather for it, sir. Name of school?"

"St. Christopher's, Pelesmith, Darlington."

"But *they* haven't sent you to London."

"No. I take it that you regard preventing crime, Sergeant, as better than apprehending a criminal after the event?"

"I don't quite follow," said the sergeant, who did.

"I'm interested in a boy called Keith Burrows. I assume you people know that he's missing?"

"Absconded, you mean? I am unable to divulge that kind of information to members of the public."

"Oh, rubbish! I'm not the public. I'm the boy's teacher."

"But you said you are on leave, didn't you, sir?"

"You don't go on leave from being human."

"So what is the purpose of your humanity, Mr. Tyson?"

Tyson reddened. "I think you're trying to rattle me."

"I'm sorry. I am only trying to establish what it is you want. Why you've taken the trouble to come to us. There are proper channels, sir. I'm sure the authorities at St. Christopher's are handling the matter at their end, as we are at ours."

The brown eyes flashed. "You mean, you know where they are?"

"*They*, sir?"

"Burrows and the other lad—Scobie. But you

haven't actually taken them into custody? Or is that something else you can't divulge?"

"Your tone is rather . . . hostile."

"Is it?" Tyson surveyed the sergeant thoughtfully. "Those channels you referred to, Sergeant—rather rigid and icebound, aren't they? You'll pick up the boys hiding out somewhere and have them packed off to Darlington."

"Anything wrong with that?"

"Maybe not, if it's that simple."

"If you are able to help us with our inquiries, sir, we shall be grateful."

"Oh, stop being so ruddy formal, Sergeant. I suppose you're wondering how I came to believe that the boys may be in this district?"

"It crossed my mind."

"There was a letter, written by Scobie's sister. She didn't put her address inside—I suppose she had her reasons, but the postmark was suggestive."

Sergeant Bowers sat up straighter. "Was she inviting him home?"

"Hardly," said Tyson with a strained laugh. "She told him to stay clear, in no uncertain terms. Scobie didn't receive it, though, before he and Burrows nipped off."

"You told your superiors at the school about the letter?"

Tyson blushed. "Actually, no."

Sergeant Bowers leaned forward a shade threateningly. "What exactly are you after, sir?"

"Burrows, of course. I want Burrows back before

123

he gets into any more trouble. The silly young fool shouldn't have jumped that wall, but if he had an irresistible impulse he should never have jumped it with Scobie."

"If he's such a paragon of boyhood," asked Sergeant Bowers, "what was he doing at an Approved School?"

"Wrongful conviction, you could call it," said Tyson, adding drily: "speaking as a member of the public, of course. But that's not the point. And so far as I'm concerned you can feed Scobie to the lions in Regent's Park, but I want Burrows clear, before anything irreversible happens."

Sergeant Bowers wasn't sure that he liked Tyson, who seemed to him arrogant, devious and presumptuous—among other things. But he felt respect for him. He himself had once given up a weekend to take a convicted burglar's two sons on a fishing trip while their mother was in the hospital.

His mind scarcely registered this memory, however, being too busy doing a small jigsaw puzzle with the few available facts: the watchman who'd seen Scobie with two other kids—one a fairly big boy almost his own height (Keith Burrows?) and a much smaller boy (???)—coming away from Stockpile's.

"What you're saying," the sergeant ventured more amicably, "is that Burrows was influenced by Scobie. It's a common enough situation—inexperienced lad egged on by a hardened tearaway. So Scobie charms Burrows into escaping with him, and now Burrows would be forced to do his bidding in order to survive.

124

We might even swing it—if nothing too serious happens."

"Your way of putting it is all right as far as it goes." Tyson frowned. "But Burrows is made of sterner stuff than that. What's more, he's the only lad I know who can keep Scobie tame."

"Now you've lost me."

"I mean, when it came to the crunch, Keith would be the one to hold Scobie back from violence. That boy is capable of murder."

The sergeant thought this over. "Very well, sir," he said, quietly formal again. "Your remarks have been duly noted. Now, if I were you, I'd catch the next train back to Darlington."

"But I've still got a week's leave."

"Then spend it somewhere else, sir. Parts of the south coast are quite mild in November."

"All I was suggesting was that we might cooperate a little. . . . Look, why are you treating me like a moron?"

"Not at all, sir," said Sergeant Bowers blandly. "Some of my best friends are morons."

Inspector Bainbridge jabbed gently at a *Solanum capsicastrum* with his pipe stem and said, referring to a certain house, "*There's* a den of iniquity, if you like."

"Yes, sir," agreed Sergeant Bowers.

"We could go through the lot in ten minutes, Sergeant. Dig them out, root and stem."

"We *could*, sir."

"But you'd rather handle it differently?"

The sergeant smiled. "Selective weed killer, I thought, sir."

His superior wandered closer to the window. "Sister Doreen did a moonlight flit with that con man— the one with more aliases than the common daisy."

"Scotland Yard are on their heels, sir."

"Leaving us with Max the Sailor and a bunch of kids," said the inspector ruefully. "I dare say you can handle them."

"Yes, sir."

"No offense, Sergeant."

"None taken, sir."

Inspector Bainbridge relit his pipe and looked out across the gray townscape beyond the broad window. "A *third* child, did you say, Sergeant?"

"A small one, sir, according to old Peters." We don't know anything about him."

The inspector shook his head. "You know something, Sergeant? I sometimes get the feeling that more kids are adrift out there than we ever imagine. Pecking away in odd places, unnoticed, unloved— nesting under the eaves, in holes and waste spaces, like sparrows."

" 'Not a sparrow falls,' " quoted the sergeant, " 'without your Father knoweth.' "

"I didn't know you read the Bible, Sergeant."

"Only we're not God, sir. No offense meant!"

"None taken, Sergeant," said Inspector Bainbridge.

20

Sprog woke very early on Friday morning. It was still dark but with that sense of impending day which makes one sit up and switch off an alarm clock, confident it will otherwise ring at any moment. Besides, somewhere above and quite a long way off came the rattle of milk bottles.

The boy's alarm clock didn't work anymore. Instead of bothering with it Sprog leaned across, saw that the boy was there under his blankets and gave him a gentle experimental shake. Had the boy only recently come home from a night's wandering he would flinch from a touch and curl himself up tighter. But the boy woke at once and the whites of his eyes flashed on Sprog in inquiry. Sprog didn't explain. He had no particular plan. It was merely that he had awakened and wanted activity and someone to share his consciousness. And he was cold. The electric fire was out.

When Sprog put on his jacket and Wellingtons the boy got dressed too. The dog woke, yawned, scrabbled and came and waited between them. As they crept toward the basement door, faint sounds of steady breathing came from the next recess.

The sky was patchy with unexpected stars, and frost silvered the pavements. Against the curb in the next street sat a fully laden milk truck. Its driver came away from a house, slid into the seat and guided the truck along, on the wrong side of the street, motor purring softly. At the next stop Sprog took a pint of milk and two eggs. The boy watched in the shadows. Sprog put the eggs into his pocket, then took them out again and replaced them in the tray. There wasn't much you could do with two raw eggs. He rejoined the boy, dug a hole in the milk top with his thumb nail, took a swig, then handed the bottle over. The milk truck purred on along the street.

Milk ran down their chins. When it was gone Sprog threw the bottle over a fence and a few minutes later the long, low roof of Stockpile's shut off most of the stars. Sprog had not intended to take the boy there. It was as if his legs had minds of their own: they wanted the boy to see, to know. Sprog stopped and said, "That's the place we done yesterday. Easy! You should see what's inside. Want a look?"

The boy looked at Sprog uncomprehendingly.

"You can get in through the skylight—it's a bit of a climb. You have to watch out for an old man and a dog. We'll have to shut *your* mutt in a shed. Will he bark?"

Without giving any other sign that he'd heard, the boy took a frayed piece of string out of his pocket, bent down and tied it loosely about the dog's neck.

"I can show you where the shed is," said Sprog.

Together they got the dog across. Never was an animal so good-natured about being dragged, heaved, yanked and cajoled. Fastening the workman's shed, Sprog told the boy what he expected to happen. It came out plain and uncomplicated. Sprog always expected the simplest outcome to any adventure and only rarely was he entirely disappointed. "I'm going up on the roof, got it? You drop over the wall and you'll see a door inside a sort of porch. Wait there and I'll open it from inside. Only"—here he allowed himself one possible complexity—"only if a geezer and a dog come round, scarper. Don't bother about me. I can look after meself."

Sprog stayed on the wall, worked his way along to the drainpipe, then climbed to the roof. The half pint of milk slopped in his stomach. He scarcely felt fear, only a mild sense of awe as if he were crawling along a whale's back. Below his straddled form the glass roof gleamed a soft metallic gray in the first shafts of dawn.

In that vast expanse of steel and glass it was harder to find the skylight than he'd expected, but eventually his probing knees hit on a small area of looseness. When he got his fingers under a metal frame it was easy enough to raise it a foot or more and crawl beneath, hanging and groping with his feet for a purchase on the topmost rack below. A few moments later he had lowered the skylight and climbed hand over hand down into the darkness.

He crossed to the first door, then through to the second, and let the boy in. "I told you—easy. No trouble out there?"

The no-answer presumably meant no trouble. For a quarter of an hour or so they stayed in there, the darkness gradually changing into a somber gray. Sprog stole only a bag of sweets and the boy was content to wander among the laden racks. He looked slightly bored and puzzled. He let Sprog give him a couple of rides on one of the rubber-wheeled trolleys, but the whole escapade fell a little flat.

"Might as well go now," said Sprog at last. "We don't want to be here when it gets light. Okay, though, wasn't it?"

The boy didn't seem too impressed. "To 'ell with you," muttered Sprog, disappointed. He'd tell Scobie, though. Scobie would be impressed.

Sprog had closed both doors, locking them out, before he realized that Scobie might not believe they had been there. And part of climbing through that roof was to show that he, Sprog, wasn't just a pretty face either. "We should have nicked something to take home—something that could only have come from there, to prove we done it," Sprog mused, half to himself and half to the boy. But they couldn't go back.

They collected the dog and shinned to the top of the wall. The police cruiser was waiting near the main gate, lights doused. Sprog practically walked into it.

The driver opened the door to get out, but when Sprog jumped down and broke into a run he slammed the door and started the motor. The boy lost his bored, puzzled air and left Sprog behind—though Sprog must have been breaking all local records.

They dodged through alleys and along short, deserted streets but the policeman knew the district backward. He put the little car through every maneuver in the book and when the darting figures vanished round their last corner he still had them in view.

He cruised into the cul-de-sac, using his headlights to flush them out. They'd vanished now, and the policeman was in a quandary. Had they gone to ground somewhere in the street, or could they have had time to make the fence at the end? If they'd managed to get that far, the cruiser couldn't hop a six-foot timber fence, the one dividing the street from the parked bulldozers.

The constable cruised up and down indecisively, steering the car from side to side to make best use of his headlights. He didn't radio in a report. There wasn't much to report—he'd not actually seen the kids coming out of Stockpile's and there had been no alarm. All the same, he decided, a search of those basements might prove worthwhile—supposing anyone could spare the time.

21

Scobie didn't have to look long at Sprog's flushed face to guess that something was amiss. He sat for a minute, cheeks bulging with the breakfast Keith had cooked, his cold blue eyes darting from Sprog to the boy and back.

"What's up?" asked Scobie.

"Nothing."

Sprog began making up his bed. Scobie emptied his mouth, strolled unhurriedly to the boy's corner, seized Sprog by the throat and threw him against the wall. "You've been chased. Who by and what for? Let's have it."

"Only a copper in a cruiser. He never saw us come here."

Scobie let go of him, wrenched the door open and went quietly up the steps.

He came back, his face livid. "Only a copper in a cruiser!" he mimicked. "He's still up there, hovering about like a wasp over a jam pot. Was you on the nick?"

"Cross me heart," said Sprog. "We—we took a gander at Stockpile's, that's all. He was waiting in the street. We never *nicked* anything, except a bottle of milk off a truck—and maybe a few sweets."

"Don't tell me you broke *in* at Stockpile's."

Sprog's pride got the better of discretion. "Through the skylight, easy! Just as I said."

Scobie hit Sprog—just once, full in the face. Sprog reeled back. He gave Scobie not tears but a vituperative stream of abuse. Scobie ignored it and went out again, and nobody knew where and for how long.

Sprog grinned crookedly at Keith, his eyes watering. The boy ate the toast and bacon Keith gave him.

Sprog took his own plate and said, dropping his bombshell, "If you're scarpering, mate, can we come with you?"

Keith started. "What makes you think I'm leaving?"

"You shouldn't talk in your sleep," said Sprog, "if you don't want everybody to know your business."

"*Everybody?*" asked Keith. He meant, could Scobie have heard him talking in his sleep?

Sprog didn't get it. His face, red on one side from Scobie's knuckle slap, held a pinched and longing look. "You're not just running out and leaving us with *him*?" This time he meant Scobie.

"You won't want to come where I'm going." Keith smiled.

"If it's a nick, it could be worse," said Sprog, but

he didn't quite mean it. "It's not that I *need* anybody."
He glanced at the boy.

"No?"

"No. I'm a loner, really."

"Yeah?"

"So is *he*, for that matter," went on Sprog. "What do you reckon's wrong with him?" The boy seemed too far off to be listening.

"His face . . . ."

"It's more than that, though. I'm not kidding, d'you know, I gave him rides on a trolley at Stockpile's and he never even laughed?"

"He hadn't got much to laugh about," said Keith, tiring of Sprog's chatter. He didn't answer Sprog's first question but hurriedly began packing his case.

There was no sign of the police car when Scobie made his second trip up the basement steps. However, he prowled around suspiciously. His fury had died away with his apprehension and if anybody had asked him he'd have said he'd forgotten about hitting Sprog.

When the car stopped beside him Scobie thought at first he'd been nicked after all. An arm shot out of the open door, grabbed him by his clothes and pulled him in.

Max drove off and said, "Take it easy, kid. We're going for a little ride around."

It was a longish drive through the rush-hour streets —not too hurried, for Max was always careful not to infringe traffic regulations.

On the way, Max talked. Somewhere at the top of Hampstead Heath he pulled off the road and produced a bag of crisps. They sat munching, looking down on the cold, hazy city and Max said, "Let's go over it all again, kid. You've been monkeying about in Stockpile's for peanuts. You're smart, but you need organization. We could make a nice little haul between us. A borrowed truck, a street market I know out of town . . . ."

"What's the deal, then?"

"Fifty-fifty, but naturally. Unless you want to cut any of the others in."

"Not a chance," said Scobie. "We don't need amateurs."

"Wise, son—very wise."

"Except . . . ," began Scobie.

"Spill it."

Scobie wished that he'd mentioned before the locks having been changed at Stockpile's so that his "open sesame" was a thing of the past. It made him feel small, having to admit it now.

Max, however, took the news calmly enough. "Okay, so you split your half with the other kid. Can he keep his mouth shut?"

"You must be joking," drawled Scobie. "Anyhow, I can get through the skylight easy, on my tod."

Max smiled doubtfully at Scobie's bulk. "You'd bust something, kid."

"There are other ways," blurted out Scobie.

"Such as?"

"That old watchman—Peters—he must have keys."

Max shook his head, making a ball of the empty crisp bag. "We don't go clobbering old watchmen, son. That way leads to trouble for sure."

"No," said Scobie, licking his lips. "I meant—*scare* him, see?"

"How—say boo?"

Scobie moved the leather sheath clear of his armpit, drew the knife slowly and offered Max a tentative smile.

Max's response was deadly cold. His eyes narrowed and he waited a moment before speaking. Then he said, "Don't flash that thing near me, son, I don't like it. Knives are for cutting bread and peeling apples."

"Okay." Scobie shrugged, putting the knife back a shade petulantly. "But you never know."

"I know," said Max.

The message Tyson got, late Friday afternoon, was typewritten and unsigned. He guessed at once who had written it, but not who had slipped the small envelope through his landlady's door. He'd almost forgotten having left the address of his boarding house at the police station.

"If you look sharp you may pick your Rabbit out of a hat at No. 12 Cyton Street—it's near the canal—or a Mrs. Murgatroyd may help you with your inquiries. Tell her you're from the Pest Disposal Department—she'll believe anything.

"Appropriate authorities will no doubt hold

you responsible for any obstruction of the due processes of the law."

"Thank you very much!" muttered Tyson. Policemen could be pompous hypocrites—but human, after all. "If you look sharp"—that meant they had information Sergeant Bowers hadn't thought it wise to disclose, and on which they expected to act soon.

The last piece of officialese was evidently intended to warn Tyson that he was to contrive some means of getting Burrows into his own custody, while leaving anybody else—including Scobie—to the attentions of the police.

Tyson got the message. He made a thin tube of this one which he used to light his pipe. It wouldn't do for it to be traced to Sergeant Bowers, or was it possible that his superior, some soft-hearted inspector perhaps, had connived at this unexpected piece of benevolent chicanery?

Eventually, just as it was growing dusk, Tyson put on his hat and coat, restoked his pipe and set out into the streets. At a newsstand he bought a local map and spent some time leaning against a lamppost studying it before striding out at a good, brisk pace toward the canal.

Keith, apart from the sleeping kids, was alone. He didn't know where Scobie was. Scobie had been restless and untalkative all day. Keith was brewing tea for one, giving his hands something to do, when he heard the footsteps at the front of the house.

The feet crunched on the pavement—not footsteps going casually by, but footsteps hesitant, pausing and resuming, then mounting the front steps. They came slowly up the steps. The knocker reverberated through the house; once, twice—then a third time after a long interval.

No answer: Mrs. Murgatroyd rarely answered knocks on the door, especially when Max was about.

Keith couldn't tell whether it was a policeman or not. He waited a minute, heart racing, then he pulled on his coat and went out, carefully up the steps, knuckles tight on the railings, trying to see round to the front door.

The feet came down, someone stooped, looked into the basement, and Keith found his own face locked into *his*! The visitor went away, perplexingly. Keith knew what he had to do. He followed, eyes screwed up in the drizzle. He followed the familiar big, shambling man to the end of the street.

By the building yard fence the feet stopped because there was nowhere else to go. The man knew he had been followed. He turned and said, "That was a bit of luck, Rabbit. I was hoping it might be this easy."

22

The basement slept. Sprog and the boy slept and the dog lay at the boy's feet, twitching, chin thrust in rough folds of blanket. Mrs. Murgatroyd's cat stayed on watch, sitting on Keith's empty bed like a small replica of the Sphinx, ears angled back as though outraged by some supersonic audacity. Her eyes watched unseen presences in the dark pools made by the buttress walls.

The cat started at the sound from the door, haunches frozen in half-flight. She saw Scobie's deceptively cumbersome form slip inside and her fur ruffled in the sudden disquieting draft.

Scobie came right in. For a second he saw the familiar basement through a pink haze. Then things began to sort themselves out; the tasseled lamp that Keith had fixed, the glowing rod of the electric heater, the black electric cord snaking up to the hole in the

floor above, the partly filled cup and half-eaten sandwich on a stained, cracked plate.

Scobie saw the neatly stretched blankets, the
packed bag at the head, the total absence of scattered
belongings. The bed space was as neat and final as a
well-kept grave.

Scobie saw the sleeping forms of Sprog and the
boy. He picked up a muddy boot and flung it. The dog
leaped up, emitting a faint, reproachful growl, and lay
down again. Sprog sat up, sleepy-eyed but alert. He
saw no more than a shadow but knew it was Scobie.

"Hey, who's bunging boots?"

"Wake up!" said Scobie. He swore senselessly.
"You'll die of sleep, mate. And tidy this place up. It's
like a fifth-rate lodging house."

Scobie resented the kids' easy oblivion, hated to be
alone with the searing pain of his double betrayal; but
he had no wish to communicate any of it to Sprog.
Sprog was nothing.

Followed by Sprog's mildly uneasy eyes he paced
up and down, kicking the food cans and crunching
packets under his feet.

"Watch it, mate," said Sprog squeakily. "Somebody
will hear."

"Who cares?" said Scobie. He vanished from
Sprog's view beyond the recess wall. Sprog lay down
again, eyes wide open. Beside him the boy hadn't
stirred, but the dog was awake at his feet, watchful.

Scobie flicked the cat away, stretched on his bed,
rested heavily on one elbow, took his knife from its

sheath and stabbed it into the box beside him. He watched it quiver erect in the firelight and thought briefly of his encounter with the man whose name he still didn't know. Scobie had hung around, waiting over an hour for him out in the cold drizzle not far from the house.

"No dice, son."

"Why not?"

"Listen," Max had said, "you ought to go straight. The way you feel about knives, son, you ought to keep as straight as a three-foot rule."

"Go and get stuffed," Scobie had answered.

But that didn't feel important anymore. Scobie was thinking back to all he had done for Rabbit. He'd looked after Rabbit, hadn't he? His burning thoughts took him a long way back almost to the night of Rabbit's arrival at the school. Green as hell he'd been, his eyes full of tears, crying for his mum like a baby who'd had its pacifier nicked. "Lay off, you lot," Scobie had told them. "The next one who touches him gets it." Like a big brother he'd been to Rabbit, and for what?

Keith came in, his face wet. When he peeled off his coat drops of water hissed on the electric heater. The dog stirred. Sprog gave him a glance but didn't speak. Keith was sure, then, that Scobie was there.

He went into the recess, saw Scobie's eyes and realized that he *knew*. He saw that Scobie, too, was still damp with the rain and he remembered the footsteps he'd heard ahead of him along the street.

Keith's heart turned over. He hadn't wanted Scobie to find out that way. "Been out?" he asked, wanting to get it over with.

Scobie said nothing for a long half minute. Then: "I've done with you, mate."

"Yeah," said Keith, and his mouth was dry.

Scobie went on, without moving: "Wait till we get back, that's all. I'm going to make it hot for you, Rabbit. You know what happens to grassers up there. You think we'll be put in different dorms because they always separate troublemakers? Don't count on it, mate. Anyway, I'll get you, they'll *all* get you, even if they put us in different countries."

The injustice stung Keith, and he knew there was no way of explaining it to Scobie. But he said quietly, trying to break through Scobie's wall of self-pity and loathing; "Nobody's stooled on you. Tyson came looking for *me*. What could I do?"

"A lousy stool pigeon and you was practically holding his hand!"

"Oh come off it."

"You *wanted* him to come. All along you wished you'd never jumped that wall, but you never had the nerve to go back. That's the trouble with you, Rabbit. No guts—nothing. Cookery suits you, mate. You wanted to have your own back on Turner, but you was hoping I'd do it for you. You wanted to be back in the nick, whining to everybody that you'd had a rough deal, sucking up to stoolie, but it's taken Tyson to pull it off for you. Where's the fuzz?"

"Eh?"

"Don't give me that! You're packed ready. You're going off with your mate Tyson, and he'll say you gave yourself up and because you squealed on me they'll go easy on you—right? As soon as you're clear this place will be swarming with coppers."

"It's not like that . . . ." began Keith, but he only then realized that it *was*. He'd not willed it, not chosen, not wanted it. And yet . . . when he talked urgently at Scobie, white-faced as he lay tensed on his bed beside the knife, Keith was talking partly to himself. "Look, Tyson's done some sort of a deal with the police, and they're not involved—not yet, at any rate. I *am* going back with him, but I didn't tell him you were with me, and he didn't ask. You can get clear, Scobie. Run, mate."

"Where to?" asked Scobie.

Keith was thinking. Tyson had told him so little. It was true that he hadn't mentioned Scobie, and whatever had passed between Tyson and the local police, letting Scobie off the hook couldn't have been part of any deal. Had Keith—unwittingly—sold Scobie up the river?

Keith pleaded, "Run, while you have time."

Scobie said, "Want me to carry your bag for you? I mean, can you do it by yourself?"

Keith said no more. He had nothing more to say. He picked up his bag. He looked round the recess, taking a long time, as if afraid he'd forget something.

His eyes fell on the knife. "I'll give you ten pence for that."

"What a hope!"

143

"Twenty."

"Get lost."

"See you, eh?" He avoided the cold, wet eyes. He avoided Sprog's faintly appealing gaze, picked up his bag and went out into the night.

23

Max could be sensitive and, as a result, mildly vindictive. He hadn't liked Scobie's knife, and he'd liked Scobie's "Get stuffed!" even less. Max was sly and bent, but not unkindly. The police knew his style: the way he slipped a window catch, picked a lock or jimmied a drawer. They knew the size of his shoes and even, owing to a youthful indiscretion, the whorls of his fingerprints. It was all neatly documented on file.

They also knew that Max never used violence on a "job." He had once abandoned a carefully planned burglary because to have carried it out would have meant silencing a dog. Max couldn't bear the thought of bludgeoning a dog with a blunt instrument, so he had fairly cheerfully let the opportunity go.

Max felt he was doing a service to society, fixing Scobie. On his way home that night he spotted the police car lurking under a lamppost in the drizzle, parked on double yellow lines too close to a corner. He tapped on the window. Cautiously, someone wound it halfway down.

Max said, "Fancy some promotion?"

"Come again?" asked P. C. Jones.

"Number Twelve, Cyton Street—got it? Don't bother to knock on the door, that'll get you nowhere. Zoom on the basement and you may find something to your advantage."

"If you would care to give me your name and address, sir?"

"I wouldn't," said Max. "But give me, say, fifteen minutes and I'll make things easier for you. Oh, and chum, look out for steel." Max went home, slightly roundabout. When he let himself in Mrs. Murgatroyd asked, "Have you any shillings? The meter's still playing up."

Max smiled and patted his mother affectionately on the shoulder. "Not to worry, Ma. It's nearly got to the end of the game."

He went softly out into the hall, opened the cupboard door and, without bothering to stoop down, yanked with his foot. The recently installed plug issued a few bright blue sparks and lay disconnected beside the dusty pickle jars.

The sudden blackout in the basement, which had happened before, caused no immediate havoc. Perversely, having slept through everything else, the boy woke and Sprog could feel his warm, familiar shape close to him in the pitch darkness.

"Power cut!" said Sprog. "Mrs. Murgatroyd's run out of shillings. The juice will come on again in a minute."

It didn't. Sprog heard Scobie swear and begin groping about. A match flamed, then went out.

"The lamp's round here," called Sprog. "I'll bring it."

He found the oil lamp and started to carry it toward Scobie's recess. The dog growled with a sudden urgency. The faint light from the street lamp, now that Sprog's eyes were becoming adjusted, outlined a moving figure—a head and shoulders against dusty glass. Sprog almost dropped his unlit lamp—the head undoubtedly wore a peaked policeman's cap.

Sprog drew back, sharp. He whispered to the boy, "It's the law, mate. Wonder if it's the same copper who chased us from Stockpile's?"

Then Sprog sensed the emptiness of the bed beside him, the absence of both boy and dog. He awaited his own chance. A powerful light beam pierced the basement, swishing every corner in turn. Sprog got under his blanket, peeping under the edge. When darkness returned he grabbed all the belongings he could find and crept toward the door. He wouldn't have made it had the policeman not been fully occupied in Scobie's recess.

Scobie had made no attempt to hide. Scobie had a knife in his hand and his eyes shone like a cornered animal's in the focused light.

"I should put that away if I were you, lad," said the

constable, trying to keep his voice steady. "You'll only make things worse for yourself."

It was a speech Scobie had heard before and would hear again—if the policeman was lucky, if Scobie was lucky. The question hovered uncertainly for several long moments—before Scobie came at him. . . .

In the early hours, Inspector Bainbridge's bedside telephone rang shrilly. "Don't you *ever* sleep, Sergeant?"

Sergeant Bowers made his report. The first part made the inspector sit straight up, wide awake with concern.

"Stabbed—how badly?"

"Nasty flesh wound, sir," said the sergeant. "The hospital says he'll be back on duty in a week. Apparently it was a near thing, though. If the man hadn't had his wits about him . . . ."

"What man?" asked the inspector sourly. "And *what* wits?"

"Er—Jones, two-three-nine, sir."

"What precisely was he doing in that basement? He wasn't there on our authority."

"No, sir. In a way I suppose he stole our thunder. I'd organized things, as you suggested, leaving time for that other lad—Burrows—to get clear."

"With the schoolmaster Johnny?"

"That part worked out all right at least. They're on the train to Darlington."

"And?"

"I don't know, sir. I suppose Tyson will keep at it till the kid's case is reviewed. . . ."

"No, I mean and *then* what happened?"

"Oh! A member of the public put Jones on to the basement. Didn't give a name or address."

"Odd!"

"Yes, sir. Jones got there and Scobie had a knife."

"Obviously! Anyone else?"

"In the basement? There were two other beds apart from Burrows's, our chaps say, and a lot of stuff probably lifted from Stockpile's . . . ." The sergeant's notebook rustled as he turned over a page. "And something about an electric meter—doesn't seem relevant. No sign of the other occupants themselves. We've got a man hanging around, but I doubt if they'll turn up —if they've got any sense. Mrs. Murgatroyd . . . ." The sergeant's voice paused.

"What about Mrs. Murgatroyd?"

"Oh, she started talking about some kid called Charlie. . . ."

"Charlie who?"

"No idea, sir. She clammed up."

"You surprise me! And Max?"

"Well, we've nothing on Max at the moment."

"Humph! Scobie?"

"Down at the station, sir. Playing it tough and cool. And sir . . . ."

"Yes, sergeant?"

"About Burrows's part in the local pilferings . . . ."

"Anybody pressing charges?"

"Only Scobie could implicate him, sir. Oddly enough, he isn't trying it on so far, even though he must believe that Burrows squealed. You'd think his friend Rabbit had . . . never existed."

They spent the night in the timber yard, high up on the planks, and when they awoke new stars winked through the cracks and a solitary bird twittered not far away.

They climbed stiffly down, Sprog just a little wary and watchful, but the yard and alleys were deserted and still.

The boy walked casually on, carrying his bag, the dog limping after. Sprog heaved his precious duffel onto his shoulder and followed—toward the soft hiss of water beneath the canal crossing. There they paused a moment looking down at the faintly lit tow-path.

Then the boy cocked a leg over the wall and climbed down the steep bank. The dog scuttled off to find an easier way, and Sprog saw the pair of them reunited by the tunnel mouth. The boy suddenly turned his face up at Sprog, a shadowed face beneath the knitted hat. Sprog nearly shouted down, but he knew how loud his voice would sound in the early silence.

He put his own leg across the wall and climbed down the embankment, nettles stinging his hands. He stood beside the boy and said, "I'm off now, mate—cheerio."

The boy looked away. Sprog went on, "I'm marked,

see? The coppers are on me tail. It's time I scarpered."
Overnight he'd convinced himself that all the police
in London had sworn an oath to get him. He felt a
little scared, a little proud.

The boy walked on several paces along the canal
towpath. He didn't look back, but the dog did—
reproachful, puzzled, waiting. "If they get me," said
Sprog, "they'll get you too. I don't want to land you
in that sort of trouble. You're better off without me."

When the boy walked slowly on, the dog stayed
where it was. It even sat down, wagging its tail
absurdly, tongue questioning. "Go on after him," said
Sprog. He called out once more, not too loud.
"Cheerio, then, see you around, eh? Ta for letting me
kip in the basement, and ta for the boots and that."

Then the boy turned. The dawn flushed, turning
the canal surface into a pink face, and the boy's face,
just for one mysterious second, caught the light and
was transformed. There were tears on it, Sprog
thought. Tears and features and expression and lonely
pleading.

"You was okay before I rolled up," said Sprog.
Then: "Trouble, that's all I am. . . . Oh, blimey!"

He sauntered toward the boy. He put an arm round
his shoulders and walked on beside him. Side by side,
along the brightening towpath, they went on, hitch-
ing up their bags.

Stiffly, as though on crutches, the dog limped close
behind them.